To: Susan Rogers

" Injustice anywhere
is a threat
to justice
anywhere."
MLK

S. Modele Clarke
5/6/19

To: Susan Rogers

"Injustice anywhere is a threat to justice everywhere."

→ MLK

Rochelle Clarke
5/6/19

STORIES FROM THE PEWS

STORIES FROM THE PEWS

G. Modele Clarke

To order additional copies of this book, contact:
Xlibris
1-888-795-4274
www.Xlibris.com
Orders@Xlibris.com
778218

CONTENTS

Contents

This book is dedicated to the Reverend Evelyn J. Clarke, my wife of forty-eight years. I thank God for her encouragement, which comprised of equal parts of truth, inspiration, and reassurance. Thanks for always keeping it real.

To the New Progressive Baptist Church (New Pro) disciples who have tolerated my *difference* for twenty-three years and have allowed me to be me.

And to Lysa Paz, my first-round copy editor, thanks again for your focused and skillful eyes.

THE TRIAL SERMON

Reggie woke up agitated. He was troubled because he went to sleep really pissed off the night before. But he couldn't remember what it was about now. He had been having these memory blackouts lately. He would try to remember something, but the memory would evade him. It was much like the string on a runaway balloon that slowly drifted just beyond his outstretched fingertips. And his head was beginning to ache from the effort.

Reggie instinctively reached over to the cluttered nightstand for a cigarette when he remembered where he was. This was his grandmother's house, where he had lived for most of his life and where smoking was forbidden. And although he had a solution for the immediate problem, the anticipated effort it required ticked him off some more. He would have to get out of bed and sit at the open window in order to empty his lungs of smoke into the chilly April air. He had been lighting up at the window ever since he was sixteen years old when he discovered the covert pleasure of smoking. So he grudgingly dragged himself to the window with an unlit Newport between his lips. He finally had something tangible to be pissed off for the first time that morning. Here he was, seventeen years later, still having to sneak a smoke in his grandmother's house.

This is some sorry crap, man. And you are one sorry dude. You know that?

He lit the cigarette, pulled a metal folding chair across the room, and effortlessly raised the window about six inches. Reggie recoiled as a blast of chilly air wafted past him. He craned his head sideways under the opening before blowing the smoke outside.

OK, man, think hard. What was it, man? What was it?

The balloons floated past his consciousness as his fingers reached desperately for one of the strings. Reggie felt he would need a drink with the cigarette to keep his frustration in check. That's when he heard Mattie

Moss Clark's voice floating up from downstairs. After a few moments, he recognized "A City Called Heaven," his grandmother's favorite Mattie Moss Clark song. Reggie snatched one of the balloon strings and pulled it down.

It was Sunday morning. Ever since he was old enough to remember, Mother Boone, his grandmother, maintained the same Sunday morning ritual. She would get up and go downstairs to the dining room to pray. Mother Boone had never learned to pray silently. So she would creep downstairs as quietly as she could because she wouldn't want to disturb the Reverend, as she called Reggie's grandfather. Then she would conduct her own prayer meeting once she got down to the dark, cluttered room. She knelt at one of the dining room chairs and spoke to God in a loud nasal chant. She always thanked him first for waking her up. That she woke up to see another day became a much bigger deal as she grew older.

"My Master, here I am, once and again, your humble servant, just want to stop by while the rest of the world slumbers and sleeps . . . I just wanna take a minute of your time to say thank you, Master. Thank you for allowing me another chance to walk in the land of the living, Master.

"My Master, there are many who went to sleep last night who can't wake up this morning. And I just want to say thank you, sir, for another day's journey.

"There's many lying in the hospital beds who, if you call them by name, can't answer, my Master. But you saw fit, because of your goodness and your mercy, to open my eyes one more time, to give me the activity on my limbs, and to wake me up this morning, clothed in my right mind. And for that, my Master, I thank you."

After she got off her knees, Mother Boone would pick through her stack of gospel records scattered in no particular order along the entire length of one wall. Once she started breakfast, she would return to her room to hang the Reverend's church clothes on a door hook and return to the kitchen.

Man, the only thing that's changed is that it's 1991, and the Reverend ain't here no more. She ain't never going to change.

So it was Sunday morning. And suddenly, it all came back to Reggie in a rush. All the earlier elusive balloons seemed to plop effortlessly into his memory. It was Sunday, and he would be preaching his trial sermon in about eight hours. He intended to stand up in his granddaddy's pulpit next door and prove to everyone that he was the rightful heir to the Holy Pilgrim Baptist Church. Rev. Major Boone built and founded that church forty-two years ago, and despite what anyone believed, Reggie presumed to be its inheritor.

Major Boone moved to Kingston, in Upstate New York, from St. Matthews, South Carolina, in 1946 as a young man. He came to work as a laborer in one of the brick factories along the Hudson River. He had few expectations when he came to Kingston. He simply wanted to escape the soul-crushing poverty he knew in St. Matthews. As a child, Major didn't know any black people there whom he considered to be well-off. But life became significantly more intolerable after the war. He came to accept that living in the rural South with any semblance of dignity was impossible for an uneducated black man.

So like thousands did before him and many thousands after, he and his young wife, Willie Mae, left the rural poverty of the South for the urban poverty of the North. He was barely literate and was a big man with hands roughened over time by the monotonous stacking and unstacking of millions of bricks. But as he said so often, he believed God had sent him up north to build a church and to lead people to heaven. He possessed absolutely no theological training and, at best, employed a very literal understanding of the Bible. But that never bothered him or his coworkers, who began gathering for weekly prayer meetings in his home on Gill Street, in the city's Ponkackie section. And over the course of three years, what started as a small stack of bricks stashed under the back porch grew into a tarpaulin-covered knoll that occupied most of the backyard. Boone literally built his church in an overgrown vacant lot next to his home.

He became Brother Boone during the prayer meeting phase and quietly and easily assumed the title of the reverend after he installed himself as pastor of the new red-bricked church. He never had patience for the formalities and rituals of Christian hierarchy to which his more conventional colleagues in the clergy seemed bound. Over the years, he neither observed nor respected any of their accepted rites of passage. He erected his church brick by brick. He built every rough uncushioned pew himself. If anyone helped, it was of their own volition. He didn't go out begging for anyone's assistance. So he wasn't beholding to any man to ordain him. And he sure didn't need them to tell him how to run his church.

"What I care about what them hypocrites say about me?" he would say from the pulpit. "They didn't call me. God called me!"

The Reverend's final abandonment of civic and collegial involvement came at a city hall gathering for dignitaries following a mayoral swearing in one frigid Sunday evening in January 1959. Willie Mae convinced him to attend the event despite his initial reluctance. He felt very ill at ease during the entire proceeding, and just before he slipped out, the pastor of one of the city's two Lutheran churches approached him and introduced himself.

Rev. Geoffrey Heinrich, who recently transferred to Kingston from Des Moines, felt an unbridled disdain for the few homegrown Negro pastors he had met in his travels. It bothered him that these barely educated men were allowed to lead worship communities. He found these pompous, flamboyant peacocks to be as uneducated as the colored people they supposedly led. And because he had recently transferred from Des Moines, the Lutheran pastor had not yet met any of the other white clergy at the reception. So Reverend Heinrich found himself standing next to Reverend Boone. But they stood together mostly because the Reverend had purposely avoided the small tight cluster of black pastors at the rear of the room. The Baptist and Lutheran pastors were like two incompatible misfits isolated in the middle of the crowd.

Reverend Heinrich didn't even bother to introduce himself. It wasn't as if he would ever socialize with the colored guy anyway. He was simply mildly curious.

"You're a pastor or something?" It sounded more like an accusation.

"Uh-huh," Reverend Boone responded indifferently, his eyes fixed on the immobile fan blades suspended from the ceiling.

"Tell me something," Reverend Heinrich said, his eyes finding the same fan. "Where do you people go to become ordained?"

"What you mean?" Reverend Boone snapped, making no attempt to disguise his irritation.

"It's always fascinated me how you colored people get your titles. I mean, is there a special seminary or something that give people like you theological degrees?"

Reverend Boone turned to look at his interrogator. It was one of the few times he had ever looked directly into a white man's eyes. He saw the smug, patronizing racism he could never abide. He turned and abruptly walked out of the building.

It was because of that persistent anger that Reverend Boone did not entertain a shred of moral anxiety about the pilfered material with which he constructed his church. And as if to settle any lingering questions about the morality or legality of his actions, he preached a few early sermons from Second Kings about God making provisions for the building of his temple. He obliquely compared himself to the young King Solomon for whom God had made preparations for the massive project.

"If it's God's will, he will make a way somehow. God made sure Solomon's daddy had saved up enough money for the job. God then went ahead and provided Solomon with cedars from Lebanon. God provided Solomon with the best carpenters, masons, and stone cutters to do the job. I tell you, if it's God's will, he will make a way somehow."

Boone preached variations of that theme for years. No one ever accused him of justifying his theft—at least not to his face—although it became the source of considerable snickering at other worship communities across the city. And if the brick factory owners ever recognized their material on the new church building, they never acknowledged it. After all, a few hundred bricks was a small price to pay for the freedom of doling out the subsistence wages they paid Boone and his coworkers.

Reggie remembered now why he awoke so pissed. It was another infuriating telephone conversation the night before with Beverly Merriweather, the church's adult-class Sunday school teacher. She had been trying to persuade Reggie to renounce his claim to the pastorate because she was better qualified than he was. And she had been telling everyone it was what the Reverend would have wanted. Bev's campaign to take over the church was subtle at first. She had been hinting about her *call* to the preaching ministry even before the Reverend died. The weird thing was that her classes had begun to sound increasingly like sermons immediately after he died in January. It started with her getting *happy* in front of the class a few times and shouting "Hallelujah" for no apparent reason.

Now everybody knew the Reverend didn't play that. All it took was one long look from him to quench any unruly spirit in the building. And dancing in the spirit was definitely not tolerated. Holy dancing folk who came in from holy dancing churches either went back to their holy dancing churches or lost the gift of dancing quick and in a hurry. But Bev discovered her dancing gift about a week after the pastor died. It was a dancing gift that required no music. The dancing spirit appeared to start hitting her more frequently as the weeks wore on. And it didn't take much for the spirit to take over her body. It might be over a single passage of scripture. A few times, the spirit commandeered her feet over some revelation she would claim to have discovered.

Like the time when it was Janice Fowler's turn to read a scripture verse from Acts 9:3. The Sunday school lesson was almost over, and the class of about twelve, mostly middle-aged church members, were relieved that Bev had not caught the Spirit once during the entire lesson. Her antics were fun at first and were an interesting distraction. To their knowledge, no one had ever caught the Holy Spirit before, especially while teaching a Sunday school class. Sure, they saw people in other churches catch the Spirit while singing or during the preaching—if the preacher was really preaching—and if the Word touched their spirit. But Bev seemed to be overdoing it lately.

Janice Fowler was a squat, plumpish woman with thick ankles and who did everything slowly and deliberately. Reading was no different. She stood up painfully and brought her battered large-print Bible a few inches from her nose.

"As he journeyed," Janice Fowler began reading methodically, as if she was testing the viability of each word, "he came near Damascus, and suddenly . . ."

"And what!" Bev shouted at her.

Janice Fowler seemed startled for a moment before she caught on.

"And suddenly."

"And what?" Bev screamed at her again.

A slow smile spread over Janice Fowler's broad round face. She knew now what Bev expected from her.

"And suddenly!" She screamed the words across the sanctuary. It was as if the women had engaged each other in a shouting contest.

"That's right!" Bev bellowed. "And suddenly!"

She began circling the lectern while rhythmically dipping her knees before jerking herself upright. It was as if she were responding to a drumbeat no one else could hear.

"Ah, shunda, haha. Oh, thank you, Lord."

Bev allowed herself a few more trips around the lectern before standing erect and placing a hand on her flat chest.

"Whew. Thank you, Lord," she said, managing to sound breathless. "Sometimes the Word sneaks up and hits me, and I just can't help myself. It's so powerful."

By this time, she had everybody's attention. Even the ancient Deacon Alex Bowen came out of his obligatory Sunday school nap to catch some of the action.

"Suddenly," Bev said, pointing a bony finger at Janice Fowler. "That's how God moves. Oh, hallelujah! Go on, Sister Fowler."

"And suddenly," Janice Fowler continued, smiling with obvious contentment that her reading evoked such excitement. "And suddenly a light shone around him from heaven . . ."

"Oh my god, Sister Fowler. What you just say?"

Janice Fowler was beside herself by this time. She was reading words that kept causing such excitement. She was having the time of her life.

"I said, 'Suddenly!'" She responded, smiling in anticipation of more accolades for her reading.

"No. No," Bev said impatiently. "What you say after that?"

"Oh," she said, a little crestfallen. "A light shone around him from heaven."

"A light, you say?"

"Yes, a light," Janice Fowler repeated, more animated now. She looked at Bev, beaming.

"Oh my god!" Bev yelled. It was as if she had opened her purse and discovered an unexpected treasure. "Y'all hear what she said? Y'all didn't hear her. What she say, Sister Marshall?"

"She said, 'A light.'"

"What she say, Brother Gerry?"

"A light!"

"Who's the light, Brother Ronnie?"

"Jesus!"

"Who?"

"Jesus!"

Then it was as if Bev heard that drumbeat again because she started dancing around the lectern. This time, she had one hand on her hip and the other outstretched, as if to take some unseen hand to steady her.

Reggie had seen that particular performance from the back of the sanctuary. He hadn't attended church much in recent years. But after his grandfather died, he thought he would show his face around Holy Pilgrim Baptist Church again. After all, the church would need some Boone leadership now that the founding pastor was gone. So he had taken to sitting in the last rows, hands spread out along the back of the pews, watching. It never occurred to him to join the class because that would be acknowledging that Bev was capable of teaching him something.

She can't teach me jack.

His grandmother asked him once why he simply sat back there, glaring at Bev every Sunday morning.

"Reggie, it going to hurt you to sit in the class and participate. You just sitting at the back every Sunday, looking all mean, like you ain't got no sense," Mother Boone said.

"Well, I have better sense than to be in Bev's class."

"Why you say that?"

"First of all, she's a fake and a phony. And second of all, she ain't got no business standing up there, acting all up and talking all that unknown tongues nonsense."

"Well, I agree she don't have to do all that. But at least she stepped up to do something when the Reverend take sick. She didn't have to do that."

"You right about that, Grandma. She didn't have to step up. But she wanted to step up. I don't know why y'all let her do all that. Y'all don't see what she doing? She just trying to take over the church."

"But, son, who was going to keep things running?"

"Anybody but not her! My grandfather would never have no woman teaching and preaching in his church!"

"You think I don't know that? But who else was ready? We was going to wake up Deacon Bowen to take over the church? Bev was like a ram in the bushes when the Reverend take sick. I, for one, is happy and thankful she stepping up and keeping things moving."

"But having a woman up there and in charge is not biblical. My grandfather never allowed it. In all the years he pastored Holy Pilgrim, he never once had a woman in that pulpit to preach, sing, teach, nothing."

"That's because he was old and stuck in his ways, son. But you, you're a young man. You don't have to be so rigid like your grandfather."

"It's not a question of being stuck or rigid, Grandma. Like my grandfather used to say all the time, if it's in the Bible, it's the Word of God. You can't just rip out the page if you don't agree with it."

"Ain't nobody saying to rip out nothing. I'm just saying that sometimes the Reverend took things from the Bible that he liked and took it too far sometimes."

"Well, he didn't take this too far. He used to always quote from First Corinthians Fourteen and verse number Thirty-Four, that women should remain silent in the church."

"Reggie, come now. You really think the Good Lord mean it like that? You standing there telling me that the Lord didn't mean for no women to say nothing in the church at all?"

Before answering, Reggie reached across the table, picked up Mother Boone's tattered Bible, flipped through several pages furiously before smacking the opened book enthusiastically.

"Here it is. Here it is right here," he said. "'Let your women keep silence in the churches, for it is not permitted unto them to speak. But they are commanded to be under obedience, as also saith the law.' That's what I'm talking about. The Bible says they are not allowed to speak."

Mother Boone looked distressed. She had been subjected to variations of this very argument with her husband over the years. And although she said she believed in the Bible's inerrancy, there were moments like this when she didn't know what to believe. She often wondered if it was really God's intention to keep women muzzled in the church. She felt drenched by a familiar wave of confusion and frustration. As with her husband, she decided to keep her opinions to herself.

Reggie sucked deeply at the cigarette before flicking it through the half-open window and watching it bounce once on the roof before disappearing into the backyard below. It frustrated him that Bev was teaching every Sunday now and that she thought she knew more Bible than he did. He was sure Bev had already developed strong support for her candidacy as pastor, especially from the Sunday school crowd. But Reggie had two decisive elements working for him that Bev did not. He had tradition and family legacy on his side.

It don't matter. This is my granddaddy's church. Even if you think you know more Bible than me, is still my granddaddy's church. Even though you holler and jump around like a drunk skunk, is still my granddaddy's church. And guess what? After you done jumping and shouting, at the end of the day, is me that'll be the pastor.

Reggie walked down the hall past his grandmother's room to go to the bathroom. He planned to get dressed and be early for Sunday school for a change. He wanted to set a good example now. He felt the people needed to be assured that after his trial sermon that evening, he would be the model of resilient Christian leadership.

For one thing, he would have to start dressing like a pastor. Currently, his worship service wardrobe consisted of one ancient navy-blue blazer of undetermined fabric and two pairs of nondescript slacks that he had been meaning to take to the cleaners. Fortunately, he had this beige gabardine suit he had been keeping under plastic for more than two years. He bought it for ten dollars from Ham-Bone, a wiry, strung out, former player pimp. He knew Ham-Bone ripped it off from the cleaners on Flatbush Avenue. But Reggie didn't care. His greatest concern was that the suit's rightful owner might recognize it and challenge him at a club or at a wedding. So he kept it under wraps for the right occasion. And today was that day. He would wear his stolen, but very fly, beige suit to preach his trial sermon.

But he would have to see about getting the church to buy him at least three new suits after his installation. He had to have a black suit for First Sundays and funerals. Then he had to have a gray suit for civic and social events in the city—not too churchy but not too fly either. But the outfit he really wanted was a maroon three-piece suit with matching alligator shoes. He had seen the outfit a few weeks earlier in a store window on Main Street in Poughkeepsie. It was as if the suit knew his name. It kept calling him back to the window for another look and then another. At the time, he had no idea where he would find sixty-five dollars for the suit and forty dollars for the shoes, plus tax. But now, he knew exactly how it would happen.

There must be a God somewhere . . .

It was about 2:30 p.m., and Reggie and his grandmother were sitting at the dining room table, going through the motions of eating an early supper. But they were both merely nibbling at the pot roast, sweet potatoes, and rice on their plates. Rev. Rufus Carrington, the interim pastor, a retired pastor from Hudson, had stopped in after the service to apologize for not being able to attend the trial sermon later and to wish Reggie well.

Mother Boone was apprehensive about the service later that afternoon. She knew her grandson felt entitled to assume the Reverend's pulpit, but she never believed he was called to preach at Holy Pilgrim or at any other church. She loved him dearly, but as hard as she tried, Mother Boone never saw a pastor's heart in Reggie. She did, however, see too much of Agnes, Reggie's mother, in him.

Agnes was always self-centered, devious, and a source of pain for the Boones from early childhood. The Reverend referred to their only child as his thorn in the side. Agnes stole from her classmates, was ready to fight anyone at the slightest provocation or opposition, and she disrespected adults indiscriminately, her parents included. No amount of spankings and, later, belt whippings seemed to tame her indiscreet choices and volatile temper.

She ran away one rainy Sunday morning in May 1961 after one of those beatings. She had walked into the house and upstairs to her room early that morning after being out all night. Agnes's attitude as she returned home was as if spending the night—God knows where—was normal behavior. Mother Boone and her husband took turns beating Agnes in her room, in the bathroom, and in every part of the house she sought refuge.

He beat her out of the rage generated by his pent-up shame. She pounded on Agnes because of her fear and frustration. Both parents retreated to their room after the beating. They were panting, shaken, and surprised by their fury and violence. The couple sat on either side of their bed in silence. They heard the front door slam moments later, but neither of them had the strength to get up.

Mother Boone often relived the agony of that Sunday morning, but particularly on Mother's Day, the anniversary of the last time she saw her daughter. She later learned that for a while, Agnes lived in Newburgh—a small city about twenty miles south of Kingston. But there was no contact with her until the Boones received an urgent phone call in November 1962. The caller, a woman, demanded they go to an address in Brooklyn. The woman refused to surrender any more information. The caller concluded with what sounded like an ominous warning.

"Y'all better come today. I ain't responsible for nothing after that."

Later that day, the Boones pulled up in front of a three-story, red-bricked apartment building on the corner of Saratoga and Sutter avenues in Brooklyn's East New York neighborhood. The IRT, elevated subway trestle that ran above Sutter Avenue, obliterated any of the day's remaining sunlight that might have brightened the gloom and systemic neglect of the street below.

They sat in the car for several minutes, trying to gather themselves before entering the building. The Reverend was clearly out of his element. The throngs of people everywhere, the heavy traffic, and the incessant city noises unnerved him tremendously. The drive from Kingston, normally about two and a half hours, took him four nerve-racking hours.

A cluttered candy store and a record store occupied the building's first floor. Sam Cooke's "Twistin' the Night Away" thundered from a cabinet speaker on the sidewalk in front of the store. As the Boones tentatively eased out of the car, the sudden rumbling and screeching of a subway train above startled Willie Mae. She ran around the front of the car and grabbed her husband's arm. And before she could recover from the terror of that ear-piercing racket, the sounds of dozens of feet racing down the subway station's metal stairs forced her to squeeze the Reverend's arm tighter. Suddenly, the Boones found themselves surrounded by multitudes of commuters streaming past, nudging, shoving, and pushing them. They were like twigs stuck on a rock while the waters of a mighty raging river rushed around them.

They apprehensively climbed the stairs to the third floor and knocked on the first of four grimy green metal doors. After a while, a rail-thin, light-skinned, young woman wearing a stocking cap opened the door. It was early evening, but she was wearing a faded-blue nightgown with blobs of food stains down the front. A pair of dirty brown bunny slippers seemed to swallow her bony feet up to the ankles.

"Y'all Small Change peoples?" she asked, her voice raspy and flat.

"Who?" the Reverend ventured hesitantly.

"I'm Barbara who called you. Sorry. Agnes. Y'all Agnes peoples," she said. "Small Change is what everybody call her."

"Yes. I'm her daddy, Reverend Boone, and this is my wife, her mother," the Reverend said.

The stench of cigarette smoke, stale urine, baby poop, and hot, dry air hit the Boones as they stepped inside the door. The stink invoked memories of the outdoor latrines they left in North Carolina. Barbara led them back out the door and down a short hallway into a stiflingly hot studio apartment. It was littered with soiled diapers, opened baby food jars, and mounds of dirty clothes. Across the room, Willie Mae saw a kitchen sink piled high with food-crusted dishes, cups, and pots. She instinctively pulled her coat tightly around her as she saw at least a dozen cockroaches scurrying boldly along the dirty countertop and among the dishes in the sink. The only light in the apartment came from a bare, grimy window above the sink.

Willie Mae heard the faintest whimper in the darkest corner of the room and turned in its direction. She saw what appeared to be another bundle of dirty clothes. But as she took a hesitant step toward the sound, the bundle of clothes turned out to be a naked baby lying in a pile of soiled sheets and blankets. She stepped closer and realized it was a boy. The infant looked up at her with expressionless eyes. It was as if he had already been disappointed so often that he didn't expect anyone to bring the faintest glimmer of light into his dark world.

She looked over at her husband and saw the muscles in his jaw quivering. Willie Mae knew she had to say something before the Reverend blew up. There were riveting questions she had to ask, although she really didn't want to know the answers. But she had to fill the silence before her husband bellowed out some angry or inappropriate remark.

"Barbara, excuse me," Willie Mae ventured. "Who place is this, and who baby is that?"

"I swear I told y'all," Barbara said, tapping a cigarette out of a box. "This here is Small Change place. I live right down the hall."

"So the baby is hers?" the Reverend said, his voice quivering slightly.

"That's right." Barbara laughed hoarsely and coughed before responding. "That there is Reggie Poop Face. Shoot. Come to think about it, I don't even know her last name, his last name, nothing."

"But where is Agnes?" Willie Mae asked, her voice beginning to crack.

"Oh, she in jail," Barbara said.

"In jail?" the Reverend bellowed incredulously. "What she doing in jail?"

"Hooking," Barbara said nonchalantly.

"Hooking? What is *hooking*?" Willie Mae jumped in, the bewilderment plainly registered on her face.

She immediately conjured up images of Agnes in a meatpacking plant, like a newsreel she once saw of aproned workers in Chicago slapping huge sides of beef and pork onto overhead hooks.

"You mean they put her in jail for working in a meat factory or something?" Willie Mae asked timidly.

"No, ma'am," Barbara answered, obviously amused by the other woman's naivety. "Hooking is like . . . Well, hooking is being a hooker. You know, a prostitute."

"Oh my god! Oh my god! Reverend, what this woman saying about our daughter?" Willie Mae moaned. She slapped an open palm to her forehead and wrapped her other arm across her stomach. She staggered a bit and would have sunk into a chair, if there was one in the apartment.

Barbara explained that Agnes was new to the business, starting a little more than five months ago, but soon after, she delivered her son. They worked as a team of sorts by helping out each other. For example, they worked the same bars on Pitkin Avenue but would alternate their time to babysit each other's children. Barbara had two young children, a toddler and a three-year-old.

"But it wasn't no good," Barbara said. "Small Change didn't know nothing about taking care of herself, much less children. I'm just being honest, y'all, but that girl was a mess. You hear me? She couldn't do nothing for herself and for that kid. After a while, it was all on me. Shoot, I have my own mess I got to deal with. I ain't got time to be her momma and my kids' momma too."

Barbara told them that because it soon became evident that she couldn't trust her neighbor to supervise the children, Agnes would have to bring in enough money to provide for both households. But because she was relatively new to the business, she got greedy and careless and mistook a vice cop for a john.

"But with Small Change locked up, God only knows for how long, I got to get back out there and do my thing," she said.

The Boones returned to Kingston with Reggie that night and never mentioned their daughter's name after that. Agnes never inquired about her son, and although Reggie knew he must have had a mother, he never asked about her.

Mother Boone rose slowly and started clearing the dinner table. She couldn't shake the heaviness in her spirit that was pulling her down all day. It was Reggie's attitude. He didn't seem to be taking this trial sermon seriously. It didn't look like he was even a little nervous. She got the feeling that he thought he was already confirmed as pastor and that the trial sermon was just a minor formality. No, something wasn't right. This trial sermon was serious business. It was the first step to taking over the Reverend's church. And if it went well this evening, then the joint board would make arrangements to get him ordained before they installed him as pastor. It was an important day for Reggie, but how come she was more nervous than he was?

"Reggie," she called from the kitchen, trying to conceal her uneasiness. "Everything OK?"

"Yeah, Grandma," he called back with a noticeable edginess to his voice. "Why you asking?"

"Just trying to make sure everything's OK, that's all."

"Why wouldn't everything be OK, Grandma?"

"I don't know. I'm just asking. I mean, your sermon all done and typed up and everything?"

"I ain't write my sermon down on no paper, if that's what you mean. Everything I got to say is right up here," Reggie said, tapping a forefinger to his head.

Mother Boone was back at the dining room entrance in a flash, a bowl of rice in one hand and a serving spoon shaking violently in her other hand. Her face was a mask of excruciating incredulity.

"What you mean you didn't write nothing down? Boy, is you serious?"

"Yes, I'm serious," he responded, just short of shouting. "I ain't writing nothing down. You know why?"

Mother Boone strutted into the room and stood across the table to face Reggie. She set the rice bowl down loudly and gripped the top of a chair tightly, as if to keep herself from lunging at him.

"Yes. Yes. Tell me, why you think you getting up in your granddaddy's pulpit to preach with no manuscript?"

Reggie pushed his chair back slightly, as if to create some distance from his grandmother's irritated grimace.

"Well, first of all," he said, sounding much more subdued, "my granddaddy never preached from no paper, and—"

"Oh my god!" Mother Boone yelled across the table. "Boy, what's the matter with you? Let's clear this up right now. Don't you ever let me hear you trying to compare yourself to your grandfather."

"But I—"

"Don't interrupt me. I ain't done. You think you know everything. That's what wrong with you. You know why your grandfather never use no manuscript to preach? You know why?"

"Because he didn't need none," Reggie offered. "He always said Jesus was the best preacher the world ever knew, and Jesus didn't need no manuscript."

Mother Boone shook her head slowly. The irritation had dissolved to sadness. She moved her hand across the top of the chair with a tenderness reserved for comfortable lovers.

"No, boy," she said with deliberate clarity. "My husband didn't preach from no paper because he couldn't read but a little bit."

Reggie's head jerked up to meet the old woman's eyes, expecting to find some trace of humor there, to perhaps discover she was pulling his leg. He wouldn't put it past her because she had pulled some pretty slick tricks on him over the years. But he could find no traces of whimsy in her, just a cold, sober sadness that troubled him.

"But what you saying don't make no sense, Grandma," he said, the distress resonating in his voice. "I can't count how many times I seen that man preach. He could quote the Bible better than anybody else. My granddaddy was the best flat-footed preacher I ever seen."

"You're right. No doubt about it. The Reverend could preach flatfoot without no paper. That's because he was a very smart man."

"Yeah, but now you're telling me the man couldn't read? I can't believe it. I used to ask him why he didn't preach from no paper, and he would tell me, all the time, that all he needed was some good scripture and the Holy Ghost to help him preach. That's all."

"Well, yes. He needed a good scripture, the Holy Ghost, and me," Mother Boone said, still stroking the back of the chair, but smiling.

"And you? What you got to do with it?"

"Me? Well, the way I see it, I had as much to do with it as the Holy Ghost," she said drily.

Mother Boone, still standing behind the chair, explained that her husband never attended to any church business on Monday and Tuesday evenings. He would get home from the brickyard at about five fifteen, and after an early supper, she would read him a passage of scripture. She said he didn't much like the Old Testament because of the long unpronounceable names. But he liked the Book of Esther and anything featuring Moses. He liked Bible stories with clear and defined narratives, like the three Hebrew boys who were cast into the fiery furnace. But by far, he derived his best sermons from the New Testament, particularly the Gospels. He found the Apostle Paul's letters too complicated and required too much interpretation.

"Because I knew what he liked, he would let me suggest what we called *a reading*," Mother Boone said. "I would go to something that the Lord would lay on my heart that morning or the night before. So I would start reading real slow. Not too much, mind you. Just enough to let him take it in. I'd be reading, but I'd also be watching him at the same time. I'd be watching his face to see when we get to a part he like."

She said that once they found a sweet verse or passage, he would say to her, "That's it right there, Willie Mae. I could do something with that." Or he might say, "Stop right there! That'll preach!"

Then, over the course of the following days, she might have to read the passages to her husband several times. He would close his eyes as he visualized the activity transpiring within the text. He often muttered under his breath as the text came alive. "My, my, my" or "Uh, uh, uh." And although she was always intimately involved in every sermon's inception and development, the final product always amazed her.

"Don't get me wrong," Mother Boone said with a softness and warmth Reggie hadn't heard in a while. "Your granddaddy couldn't read worth a lick. But let me tell you something. He was an anointed preacher. That man could bring the Word. You hear me? He could bring it."

"I know he could preach, Grandma," Reggie said, almost apologetically. "I listened to him preach my whole life. I'd see him stand up in that pulpit, and I'd just tune in on him. Even as a little kid, I don't know how, but he would hold my attention. Even today, I can still remember some of his sermons. They stuck with you. But I can't say the same for most preachers. That's why I always wanted to preach like my granddaddy."

"Well, I hope you realize now that your granddaddy didn't just get up in the pulpit and preach," Mother Boone said. "He prepared, he prayed on it, and then he went and prepared some more. And you want to know why he spend almost all week on his message, Reggie?"

"Yeah, why?"

"The Reverend work hard like that because he knew his limits," she said emphatically. "And that's the problem with a lot of them young preachers today. They don't know their limits. They think all they got to say is 'God call me to preach!' And just like that, they think they is preachers."

Two hours later, Reggie was seated in the preacher's chair on the pulpit with Deacon Alex Bowen, chairman of the deacon board, in the chair next to him. The older man looked visibly uncomfortable because it was his first time seated on the pulpit. That was because Reverend Boone never allowed laypersons or women on his pulpit. But because no other clergy accepted their invitation to witness this trial sermon, the church's joint board, after considerable debate, agreed it would not be proper to have the licentiate sitting up there alone. So it fell on Deacon Bowen to sit in the other pulpit chair and to introduce the preacher. It was all he could do to stay awake with a stifling heat hanging over the pulpit. Reggie wore his beige suit. It was a little tighter than he remembered, so he left it unbuttoned.

The small crowded sanctuary was brick-oven hot. A single electric fan, set up near the vestibule at the rear of the room, buzzed noisily but did little to send any relief up to the pulpit. Sister Beulah McDavid, who looked like she was poured and stuffed into her starched white usher's uniform, had long since run out of fans. People were fanning themselves with handkerchiefs or flapping their fingers to their faces like birds with inverted wings. On the few occasions that the church was ever full, Holy Pilgrim members were reminded that the Reverend did not construct this building with ventilation as a priority. And no one dared open any of the windows to let in some of the cool spring-evening air. Logistic decisions like that were always left to the pastor, and since he was no longer there, no one wanted to assume the responsibility.

After the devotional period, which New Pilgrim deacons led, it was time for the evening's main event. Deacon Bowen got up, took a few short steps to the podium, and mumbled an invocation. He then squinted at a scrap of paper up there before inviting Trustee Janice Fowler to welcome the congregation to the service. She, in turn, announced that Brother Ronnie Lambert would deliver the obligatory statement of purpose. These perfunctory appendages to the service limped along as people secreted buckets of sweat in the tight, airless room for what seemed like forever.

But then nothing happened. There was only the sound of flapping fans and the congregation's nervous murmuring as they wondered what was supposed to happen next. Eventually, Sister McDavid walked up the center aisle, her starched white uniform swishing with every step. She stopped just short of the platform and whispered to Deacon Bowen loudly enough for almost everyone to hear, "Deacon Bowen, look at your paper. Is time for Deaconess Whitehead to read the scripture."

Deaconess Lulabelle Whitehead was already in place at the portable podium, her Bible open and ready by the time Deacon Bowen got up to announce her. But she knew better than to begin reading before being properly announced.

"The scripture is coming from Matthew, Chapter Nine and Verse Number Thirty-Six," Deaconess Whitehead said brightly. "And the preacher ask us read up to verse number 38. When you have it, say amen."

After a few moments of page shuffling and a scattering of amen across the sanctuary, she began. "But when he saw the multitudes, he was moved with compassion on them, because they were faint, and were scattered abroad, as sheep having no shepherd. Then he saith unto his disciples, 'The harvest is truly plenteous, but the laborers are few. Pray ye therefore, the Lord of the harvest, that he will send forth laborers into his harvest.' May the Lord add a blessing to the reading of his Word."

Reggie had heard his grandfather preach a sermon from those Matthew, Chapter Nine verses about twelve years earlier. He remembered how Reverend Boone used as a sermon title, "What Happens When Sheeps Ain't Got No Shepherd." The sermon reinforced Reggie's conviction that churches needed the kind of strong leadership that only men could provide. His grandfather compared church members to docile, gullible sheep always at risk of being deceived by spiritual predators. He intended to replicate that meaningful sermon as a subtle but hopefully effective suggestion to Holy Pilgrim that they would receive from him the same strong leadership that his grandfather provided.

Then it was Sister Gwen Marshall's turn to sing the song of sermonic preparation. Sister Marshall relished the moments that allowed her to dominate the church's attention. Since New Pilgrim never enjoyed the luxury of musical accompaniment, individual loudness became the musical culture—on the order of the loudest shall lead. Sister Marshall would never be accused of possessing anything near perfect pitch. But she was uncompromisingly loud. Consequently, she inherently took possession of any congregational song at New Pilgrim. That's how it was. Pastor preached, Deacon Bowen prayed, and Sister Marshall possessed the songs.

A robust woman, she stood up and sashayed from her seat to stand directly under the podium. She wore a lime-green satin-like dress that must have been too small even when she first wore it ten years earlier, a bright-yellow pillbox hat with a matching yellow feather swaying above, and sturdy pumps covered in the same material as the dress. It was her official grand-occasion ensemble. Someone offered her the church's only microphone, which she declined with exaggerated animation.

"I don't need no mic!" she bellowed, only to add, "Y'all have to excuse me today. I have a little cold, so pray for me."

Church regulars knew the routine.

"When they came to me and asked me to sing today, I didn't know what the Lord would have me to sing." She purred demurely. "So I prayed on it, and the Lord gave me this."

Sister Marshall placed one bejeweled hand on her equally bejeweled chest and thundered, "Blessed assurance, Jesus is mine / Oh what a foretaste of glory divine . . ."

Some of the uninformed in the pews attempted to accompany her on this familiar church song, only to be left in the dust as she rapidly changed keys, until she was left alone to solo in a musical stratosphere where she reigned supreme and unchallenged. Deacon Bowen, borrowing a bold move from the Reverend's playbook, finally stood up and shuffled to the podium after several agonizing minutes of Sister Marshall's "Blessed Assurance." She must have felt his presence behind her because she brought the song to an abrupt end.

"Let's give Sister Marshall a hand for that song," he mumbled as a scattering of tepid applause rose from the broiling sanctuary.

"And now is time to hear from the Lord," Deacon Bowen said. "We come from near and far to hear what the Lord place in this young man's heart."

"Amen!" came from a voice in the congregation.

"Most all of us know this young man because we watch him grow up right here in this church. As you know, his granddaddy was the founder and pastor of this church for, yeah, forty-five years, until the Lord called him home."

"Amen!"

"Well, I don't know about the rest of you," he continued, "but I wasn't too surprised when Reggie Boone say he was called to preach and that the Lord want him to take over his granddaddy church."

"Amen!"

"So the joint board had a meeting, and we decide to let the young man preach his trial sermon in front of all of y'all."

He was finding his deacon voice now. The droning monotone was giving way to a melodic, rhythmic chant.

"Oh, we don't know, huh, if this young man can pray like Peter, huh, or preach like Paul, ha. We don't know, huh, if this young man, huh, can lead his people, huh, through the wilderness, huh, like Moses, ha. All we know, huh, is what he say, huh, that God call him, huh, to preach the Word, ha. So I say to you today, young man, huh, if it is the Lord who call you, huh, preach the Word, huh, preach the Word, huh, in season, huh, and out of season, ha."

With that, Deacon Bowen fished a long white handkerchief from a hip pocket, wiped his sweaty head and face, turned around, and shuffled back to his seat. The applause from the congregation was palpable as some people jumped to their feet while others waved holy hands. It took several seconds for the noise to subside.

"I wet the ground for you, young fella," Deacon Bowen leaned over and whispered to Reggie. "Now go on and see what you can do with that."

Reggie rose slowly, almost reluctantly, from the preacher's chair and took four deliberate steps toward the podium.

This is your shot, man. This is it. You have everything riding on this.

He stood immobile for a moment, his eyes fixated on the wobbly fan at the back of the sanctuary. Although he felt the scrutiny of every eye in the room, he was not quite ready to return their gaze. Reggie, without looking down, felt his grandmother's penetrating anxiety. He also felt the apprehension coming from the pews in the broiling sanctuary. He fought the urge to look down at the second-row aisle seat—Mother Boone's designated place for more than forty-five years. He was suddenly afraid that he wouldn't find the look of reassurance and approval he so desperately needed from her. Reggie was not aware that he needed his grandmother's encouragement before that moment. It was a sobering revelation.

Oh, c'mon, man. You don't need nobody to lean on now. You got your granddaddy spirit with you, and he sure nuff bring the Holy Spirit with him. You going to be all right, man.

The applause gradually faded to silence. Someone coughed, and it was immediately answered somewhere else in the room, like frogs across a pond staking out their turf. Then the silence of anticipation commandeered the sanctuary again.

All right, all right. First thing, remember your protocol.

Reggie finally tore his eyes away from the fan and surveyed the width of the back row on both sides of the aisle. That's when he saw Bev sitting at the far end of the last pew near the aisle. She wore a shimmering gold lamé jacket over a white dress and a gold beret with white sequins pulled down over one side of her head. One hand cupped her chin as she stared raptly at Reggie.

"First of all, I want to thank Deacon, er, Bowen for that introduction," Reggie said. His voice sounded uncharacteristically hoarse and congested. "And I want to thank the joint board for giving me this opportunity today. I believe it's what my granddaddy would've wanted."

"Amen."

"Amen."

"And I also want to thank my grandmother for her support," he said, looking at Mother Boone directly for the first time. "And all of y'all for coming out this afternoon."

OK. OK. You got the protocol out of the way. Now let's go. Don't worry about nothing.

"Ahem. I want to thank Deaconess Whitehead for reading the scripture. I want y'all to look at verse number, er . . . verse number, am . . . am, verse number 38 . . . I mean, am, verse 36."

C'mon now. Keep your head in the game. Focus. Focus.

"Ahem. Where it say how they was scattered about with no shepherd," Reggie said. He became aware of a faint constriction in his throat. "Ahem. Ahem. And if I was to give this a title, I'd call it, 'Sheep Getting Scattered Without No Shepherd.'"

Reggie suddenly felt very vulnerable, standing behind his grandfather's pulpit in his tight beige suit and empty-handed. He realized that he was standing before an expectant audience with no Bible and no prepared manuscript. He wondered if this was how Jean-François "Blondin" Gravelet, the tightrope walker, felt before he went across Niagara Falls for the first time in 1859. Reggie had seen a television documentary about the French daredevil days earlier.

C'mon, man, c'mon. You can do this!

"Sheep getting scattered without no shepherd," he repeated.

"Take your time," someone called out.

Reggie tried desperately to focus, to remember his opening statement, to pull the sermon from his brain, and to feel his grandfather's presence. He envisioned the dangling strings of those elusive balloons floating across his consciousness again. He heard Deacon Bowen shift in the seat behind him before he said, "All right now, son. Preach this thing."

Help me, Holy Ghost. Help me, Granddaddy. Help me, Holy Ghost . . .

He looked down at his grandmother and quickly looked away as he saw the agony on her face. The pain Reggie saw reflected there instantly obliterated from his mind any residual traces of the sermon. He stood there, his hands tightly gripping the sides of the podium, transfixed in his bewilderment and as motionless as Lot's wife.

A solitary dry cough echoed across the room. Only the electric fan interrupted the morbid silence as it continued to buzz feverishly, stubbornly propelling hot air into the sanctuary.

Suddenly, there was clapping from the rear of the sanctuary. Every head craned backward to see who had interrupted the wretched tranquility of the moment. It was Bev. She was on her feet, walking slowly and purposefully up the center aisle, hands raised high, clapping.

"Praise the Lord, saints," she shouted, with an exuberance that challenged the sanctuary's melancholic mood.

"Come on and praise the Lord," she continued, apparently oblivious to the bewildered looks she attracted. "This ain't no funeral."

Eventually, the sound of one hesitant round of applause joined Bev's as she continued to walk toward the pulpit. It was joined by another and almost instantly by another until clapping reverberated throughout room. Although no one quite knew why they were clapping, the sound of so many hands creating such deafening applause gradually dispersed the cloud of catastrophe hanging over the room.

Meanwhile, Deacon Bowen walked toward Reggie, took him gently by the elbow, and escorted him off the pulpit. Although most eyes were focused on Bev's passage toward the pulpit, Mother Boone did not miss Reggie's inconspicuous exit. The elderly deacon silently led Reggie down a narrow hallway and past the pastor's study. He opened a side door to the small unpaved parking lot and stepped aside to let Reggie out before closing it quietly but firmly.

Reggie felt numb as he walked mechanically on the crushed gravel, one hand brushing against the building's bare brick wall for support. He stopped as he approached a window, reluctant to be seen from inside the church. He slouched against the wall and eased his body to the ground, feeling the bricks' roughness grab and pull at his suit.

After a while, Reggie could hear muted applause from inside the building. He recognized Bev's annoying nasal voice, but he could not determine what she was saying. Then there was more clapping and Bev's voice again. Even from his isolation in the parking lot, it was evident to Reggie that the mood inside had changed drastically. There was no doubt that the people were avidly receiving Bev's message.

Reggie rose slowly to his feet and walked sluggishly along the wall toward the house. He was too traumatized to care if anyone from inside saw him. He reached into a jacket pocket for his Newports.

#

THE RELUCTANT BISHOP

Rayon was about to hurt someone in a few minutes. But his detachment from the violence he was about to inflict bothered him.

It used to be that he would be apprehensive in the days and hours leading up to a beatdown of another inmate. He would minutely choreograph every detail of his attack, the execution, and his exit. His acquaintances assumed that his quick and clean accomplishments were skills gleaned from his years of experience on the street. He encouraged them to believe he existed in a volatile environment before his incarceration, where his survival depended on controlled anger and a solid reputation for viciousness.

But Rayon didn't come from the street. He learned to fight in prison. And he discovered that unbridled anger was a liability. It's why he was in prison. Also, that kind of anger breeds recklessness. It limits the fighter's success to the available resources of strength, grit, and determination. And he realized that spontaneous combat relied too heavily on spectator support. He didn't want to depend on the crowd because he wanted to control as many variables as possible when he fought. So he learned the political and social value of winning fights. Fighting in prison was all about winning. And consistent winning here was invaluable to maintaining and elevating one's public status.

However, Rayon had stacked up so many wins over the years that he believed he was becoming complacent. He had convinced so many younger men of his invincibility that he was concerned he might start believing the hype. This perception of invulnerability had become the most reliable form of currency in his world. It bought him respect. While he didn't know every inmate in Coxsackie Correctional Facility, he was sure they knew him, or they damn sure had heard of him.

Rayon came into the system bitter and combative eight years ago. He read conspiracy and potential treachery into every look, every accidental collision, or every perceived act of disrespect. And he bristled incessantly because he couldn't challenge the correction officers, but he would redirect his anger to the next available inmate. Consequently, fights were inevitable. They were mostly quiet, private affairs where the offending party would find himself fending off an unexpected barrage of blows in a mysteriously deserted bathroom. It was never about the honor and glory of defeating an opponent in a fair fight for Rayon. His days of respecting justice and fair play were long gone.

Those were honored sentiments from another season of his life. It was the season when God dominated his life. During that earlier season, he felt the blessings and love of God in his life daily. His favorite greeting for many years was "New day, new blessings." And he did consider himself abundantly blessed. He was a gifted organist who had been playing the M3 Hammond at his father's church since he was twelve. He was an ordained minister with an advanced theological degree and was one of the region's youngest bishops. That's because immediately after graduation, his father, Overseer Julius T. Hendricks, installed him as pastor of the Solid Rock Everlasting Temple in Middletown, New York, one of the churches under his supervision. And just four years later, Rayon inherited the flagship church, Bread of Life Fellowship Ministries in Newburgh. The pastoral appointment to the mother church came after the Pentecostal Apostolic Ministries of America appointed his father supervisor of the New York, Mid- and Lower-Hudson Region. He married Shantel, the love of his life, and had a son, Emanuel, before his world fell apart.

There was a path he had been diligently following before his life disintegrated. Life had a purpose then. Justice and fair play had meaning before his wife deceived him, before the system failed him, and before God abandoned him. There was a purpose to his life before everything, and everyone he trusted eventually failed him.

Rayon should have seen through Shantel's deception years ago. But it wasn't until after the troubles that he realized that everyone else had seen what he was unable to. She was an attention junkie, and he unconsciously fed her habit. He knew he loved her when he first saw her. He was playing the organ while she sang with the choir at her church's anniversary service. Their fathers had been colleagues in ministry and had reciprocal church anniversary arrangements for decades.

But this was the first time Rayon had noticed the grown-up, elegant Shantel Hill. She was the tallest choir member and possessed a presence that demanded attention. Her long straight hair formed a stunning backdrop for the most slender neck Rayon had ever seen on a real-life woman. Although he couldn't distinguish her voice from the twelve other choir members, he imagined it had to be a silky, smooth soprano with the vibrancy of a pipe organ. He found out later that it wasn't. After the selection, as Shantel filed out with the choir, Rayon observed how she seemed to glide down the aisle with a distinctive rhythm and grace. He knew even then that Shantel would be the center of his attention.

It was May 1995 when they were both eighteen and preoccupied with planning for college in the fall. They saw each other constantly that summer. And the fact that both sets of parents calculatingly encouraged their dating made those the three most blissful months of Rayon's life. Everything seemed to be falling into place for them. He had received a football scholarship to play for the Bantams at Trinity College in Connecticut. Shantel was also excited about relocating from Beacon to Le Moyne College in Upstate Syracuse, New York, where she was going to study marketing and play softball. Rayon went to see her play whenever he could during their four-year long-distance courtship.

The prediction at both churches was that Shantel and Rayon were destined to be married, and the sooner the better. No one wanted a pregnancy scandal between the churches. Several people already knew they spent whatever weekends they could together. And Rayon would always make the four-hour drive from Hartford to Syracuse whenever Shantel had a home game. He marveled unfailingly at her graceful skill and arresting attractiveness even under the most grueling conditions. He learned, during those games, that she had the exceptional ability to play hard and still look radiant. She made it appear like she was filming a television commercial.

They were married in 1999, a month after graduation, in a lavish June ceremony in which both fathers, Superintendent Julius T. Hendricks and Apostle L. Arthur Hill, presided. The marriage united two of the most prominent Pentecostal dynasties along the Hudson River. And for a while, the union enabled a seamless symmetry between their congregations.

Every day was indeed bringing new blessings. In a unique demonstration of unity and commitment, both sets of parents collaborated to buy the couple a two-bedroom condominium close to the Beacon Train Station. The plan was to make it as convenient as possible for their respective commutes to Manhattan. That was because Shantel quickly landed a job at Davidson, Engelman, and Boyd—a midsize advertising firm on Lexington Avenue, where she had done a summer internship program during her junior year.

And although Rayon was already installed as Solid Rock's full-time pastor, he commuted to the city three evenings each week to a master of divinity degree program at New York Theological Seminary. He wished, however, that he could conjure up a little more passion for his ministry.

His hermeneutics were textbook perfect. His professors would be proud of his exegesis proficiency. His preaching was consistently convincing, if not authentically fervent. But it seemed like that moment of genuine preaching passion continued to evade Rayon. It was a few months into his incarceration that he realized the passion for ministry was never his. That passion belonged to his parents and to the church members who watched him grow up at Bread of Life Fellowship Ministries.

Just short of a year after the wedding, Superintendent Hendricks and Apostle Hill announced to their respective congregations that they were going to be grandparents. The jubilation was palpable as church folk speculated on the intricacies of the interfamilial dynamics. And on both sides of the Hudson River, discussions simmered about the potential power the child would inherit. That was because the Hill-Hendricks dynasty already controlled six churches among them, and the prospects for growth was evident. But Rayon never experienced the exhilaration of anticipating a life devoted to ministry and the prospect of being the bishop of several churches.

In his moments of solitude, particularly those periods set aside for prayer and reflection, he fantasized about playing and singing at the Blue Note Jazz Club in Greenwich Village or being on tour at jazz venues across the country. He painstakingly created a full-color poster in a graphic arts class during his sophomore year at Trinity College. The poster announced, "Ray Hendricks at the Blue Note." He kept it on his wall briefly in college, but because it attracted too much attention and unwanted questions, Rayon folded it into an unused briefcase, where it has remained. Rayon fed his craving for jazz and rhythm and blues by maintaining an extensive, clandestine collection of tapes—and later CDs—of organists such as Billy Preston, Booker T. Jones, Jimmy McGriff, and his cherished Smith collection of Jimmy Smith and Dr. Lonnie Smith. However, he immediately transferred his secret passion for jazz to impending fatherhood as soon as he found out about Shantel's pregnancy.

But Shantel was ambivalent about her pregnancy and impending motherhood role from the beginning.

"I don't know, Ray," she confided one night as they turned down the bed. "After all the excitement about the baby and all of that, I guess everyone's more psyched about it than me."

"What do you mean?" Rayon responded, solemn and mildly alarmed. "I thought you were happy that we're pregnant?"

"What do you mean *we're pregnant*?" Shantel said sharply, as she looked fiercely across the bed at him. "What's this *we're pregnant*? *We* ain't pregnant! I'm pregnant! I'm the one who's going to be carrying around a big belly for the next six and a half months."

She switched off the light on her nightstand, abruptly got under the sheet, and turned toward the wall. Rayon stood on his side of the bed for a moment, puzzled and anxious. The unprovoked outburst was a new element to the relationship. He climbed onto the bed, crawled on his knees toward Shantel, and attempted to put his arms around her. But she shook her shoulders free of his embrace.

"C'mon, Shants," he pleaded. "Don't be like that, please."

"Like what?" she shot back. "Don't be honest and tell you what I'm feeling?"

"I'm sure what you're feeling is pretty common. I'll bet lots of first-time mothers get a little apprehensive."

Rayon tried to squeeze her shoulder, but she brusquely sat up in the bed, wrapped her long slender arms around her knees, and drew them to her chest.

"I'm not getting this," Rayon said with a mixture of concern and frustration. "I thought you were as happy as I am about the baby?"

"Oh, I know you're happy," Shantel snapped. "You're happy. Your mom and dad are happy. My mom and dad, they're happy. The churches, everybody's happy. Well, good for all of you."

"Shants, what's going on? Did something happen?—"

"I'll tell you what's happening," she interjected, turning to give him a look that appeared close to disdain. "I told you I was pregnant, and pretty soon, everybody was in on it. They're all beside themselves with joy. All of y'all just assume I'm beside myself with joy also. Did any of y'all stop to ask me how I feel?"

Shantel was sobbing by then. Rayon instinctively moved closer to hold her, but she waved him away.

"I just assumed you'd be the happiest of all of us," Rayon said.

"You just assumed," she said, dripping with sarcasm. "Did you assume that I would be the one with this big gut getting bigger and bigger on me? Did you assume that I would be the one getting all fat and out of shape? Did you assume I would be the one with the fat ankles and varicose veins? I didn't think so!"

Rayon suddenly realized that Shantel was not concerned with the discomforts or ailments that some pregnant women suffer, such as nausea or morning sickness. She actually never experienced any of the typical pregnancy illnesses or discomforts.

"Hold up. Hold up," he said. "You telling me that you're hung up on how you'll look while you're pregnant? That's what this is about?"

"Yes!" she said, obviously relieved. It was as if they had finally reached common ground. "Yes. Don't you see? While everybody's getting all worked up about the baby, I'm the one who'll be running around looking like a stuffed pig."

Rayon couldn't believe what he was hearing. He locked his fingers behind his head and stared at a section of bare wall in front of him. His confusion had already morphed into exasperation, on its way to anger. But he didn't want to go to there. His limited experience with his own anger had been dark and frightening. He consciously fought to avoid crossing over.

"Shants," Rayon said, with all the gentleness he could muster, "don't you think that attitude is a little superficial?"

That night represented an abrupt turning point in their relationship. Although she carried the baby, it was Rayon who bore the brunt of prenatal responsibilities. He woke up to feed the baby at night, responded to every cough or sneeze, and kept track of pediatric appointments. In addition, he made sure Shantel made her doctor's appointments, exercised, and stuck to her diet. Rayon didn't know it, but Shantel worked out fanatically when he was away. Her vanity would not allow her to accumulate unnecessary weight. However, she felt obliged to keep up the pretense of moping around the condo, being sedentary, and eating junk. But she continued to complain incessantly to Rayon about her distorted body.

If the Hills and Hendricks had their way, they would have celebrated Emanuel's birth with the same fervor the nation reserves for its Independence Day festivities. But what the families lacked in parades and fireworks, they more than made up for in pictures, videos, phone calls and emails. For weeks after, the grandfathers found ways to weave Baby Emanuel into their sermons. Rayon believed he behaved with more subtlety than the child's grandfathers, but he found it increasingly more difficult to conduct a conversation without mentioning some new astounding feat his infant son had performed. Every squint of the nose warranted a picture. Rayon saw evidence of the baby's genius in every facial expression or involuntary gesture.

Meanwhile, Shantel had become preoccupied with getting back to the gym and returning to work. For one thing, Emanuel did not suffer for childcare—not with two contending and fawning grandmothers. So less than three weeks after giving birth, she convinced everyone she was more than ready to get back to work. She effortlessly resumed her Metro North commute to Grand Central Terminal and her five-block walk to her office on Lexington Avenue and Forty-Seventh Street. It became apparent, however, that on her first day back, she had to fake serious bouts of separation anxiety. That was because several veteran mothers told competing horror stories of guilt and about close decisions to quit their careers when they had to leave their babies in childcare. Shantel actually tried, but she could not conjure up any feelings of guilt for being away from Emanuel all day.

She received a call from her mother-in-law the first morning back that convinced her to at least make an effort to play the role of a guilt-ridden mom more convincingly.

"Shantel."

"Hi, Mom. What's up?"

"Well, I knew you'd be worried sick about Emanuel by now."

"Why?"

"You know, being away from him for the first time. Don't you miss him? Aren't you just worried sick? I know I would be."

"Oh, yeah. It's kinda tough. But I have so much catching up ...—"

"Well, don't you want to know how this little fella is making out without his momma?"

Shantel wasn't sure, but she thought she detected a hint of incredulity in her mother-in-law's voice. She would have to do a better job in the future of camouflaging her indifference.

Getting her rhythm back at the agency after a two-month absence was not as difficult as she had anticipated. Patsy, the agency's creative director, brought her in as a copywriter on a new project for a coconut water brand. The client's only directive was to avoid tropical beach clichés at all costs. So Shantel spent her first day back in a glass-enclosed conference room with four colleagues gloriously pitching ideas. She sat near the center of the large oval glass-topped conference table, feeling like the new kid in the class as ideas and concepts swirled above and past her. She already knew three of the people around the table and was pretty much familiar with their creative limits. But she wanted to get a feel for the new guy. Shantel never met him before and wanted to get a sense of his ingenuity before venturing out.

His name was Vincent, and he was the only other black person in the room. When he did speak, Shantel found his suggestion of an oasis with a lone coconut tree in the middle of a desert to be quite banal. He impressed her as being creatively deprived but contemptuous and dismissive. It was as if he was a major league player doing time in the minors. But she found this strangely attractive. Vincent was rail thin, and the tight-fitting clothes accentuated his slenderness. He wore a head full of short twists and big black-framed glasses that he constantly, almost unconsciously, pushed back against his forehead.

After an hour of nonproductive banter, the team broke for lunch, and Shantel and Vincent intuitively remained in the conference room. He apparently didn't want to indulge in the inevitable small talk with the creative team as they walked down the hall; she had hoped he would hang back and give her a chance to size him up as a possible ally. She quickly learned that Vincent didn't possess an ounce of congeniality and that he evaluated most situations as they related to his well-being.

"So what'd you think of those jokers?" Vincent asked just as the last of the exiting trio stepped into the hallway. "I swear it's like kindergarten all over again."

"Well, it'll take a minute for all of us to work as a team," Shantel replied cautiously. "We're all still in the phase of checking one another out."

"Let me tell you something, little girl," he said, leaning back in the chair. "I don't know about you, but I ain't got the time to be waiting to check nobody out. You feelin' me?"

"No, you didn't!" she responded, rearing back in her seat. "You actually called me little girl?"

"Don't worry about it," Vincent said, waving his hand in dismissal. "The thing is, we have to snatch this project from these three dumb white people and make it ours."

"Hey, hold up, man. You don't even know me like that. Plus, you going just a little too fast for me. We're supposed to be a team. Patsy don't play that. When we go in to see her tomorrow, she'll want to know what the *team* came up with."

"See, that's your problem right there, little girl. You're all worried about what Patsy will say when you should be focused on how long before you take Patsy's job. That's where your head should be. You feelin' me?"

"You are off the chain, man. You just got here, and you're already thinking of taking our creative director's job?"

"That's right, baby girl. White folk have been eating high off the hog ever since we had to deal with them. And we're so used to eating the lower parts of the hog and the leftovers that we've become comfortable with accepting whatever they throw at us. But not me, girlie girl. I plan to eat as high off the hog as these white people. Hang with me, and you'll never eat pig tails and pig feet ever again."

But despite her initial revulsion to his outrageous ambitions, Shantel found herself attracted to Vincent's audaciousness. She studied him intently over the next weeks, grudgingly admiring his self-confidence. It became apparent to her that his audacity compensated for what he lacked in actual creative skills. And it seemed to intimidate their teammates because it wasn't long before Vincent became the team's unchallenged pitchperson. He skillfully consolidated the best ideas, determined the consensus, and was able to package their efforts into coherent presentations to Patsy. Shantel's respect and admiration for the barely talented Vincent increased with every successful presentation.

A little more than a month after their first conversation, their coconut water television commercial account went into production. And Vincent was getting the star quarterback treatment on the Twenty-Second Floor. Despite her increasing regard, Shantel deeply resented not receiving the full measure of attention and adoration that Vincent attracted so effortlessly. Whatever kudos she received was shared with the team's other members. But she desperately craved the individual attention the Twenty-Second Floor reserved for Vincent.

He was riding high, just as he said he would, and she wanted to experience that elevated ride. However, she would need the cooperation of her teammates to unseat him. But Shantel knew they were too intimidated by Vincent's urban street image to join her in any conspiracy. She eventually concluded that she would have to take him up on his offer to form a two-person coalition against the three other weaker members of the creative team.

They were eating lunch at a pizzeria on Lexington Avenue when Shantel reintroduced the partnership discussion.

"So what part of the hog are you eating now?" Shantel asked.

"I'll tell you one thing," Vincent responded. "It ain't the tail, and it ain't the feet."

"Why you say that?" she asked, mildly curious. "They put something new on your plate since the last time I looked?"

"Why you even looking at my plate?" he asked briskly, his mood shifting abruptly.

"Well, I only meant if something had happened since we turned in the coconut account. Why you so edgy?"

"I thought you heard something," he said, pushing his glasses against his forehead.

"Heard what?"

"Well, Patsy came to me with something in confidence the other day."

"What, and you didn't say anything to me?"

"Excuse me, missy, but since when I have to tell you anything? It ain't like that with us. I told you we could team up, but no. You want to hang all by your stuck-up self."

"So what if I told you I totally want to partner up with you to lead the team?" she said, leaning over the table between them, in what she hoped would be a gesture of seduction and surrender. "Maybe I'm ready to do this."

"But see, little girl," Vincent said, stirring his ginger ale with a straw. "I really don't need you or your partnership now. I got Terry, Jeffrey, and Beth where I want them. You know those white folk scared of me, don't you? They ain't about to get in my face. So I got this."

Shantel could feel her place on the hog food chain slipping away from her. She knew she had to stick with Vincent if she was to enjoy the attention and recognition she craved.

"Oh yeah?" she shot back. "You think Jeffrey, Beth, and what's-her-name a little scared of you now? Well, they've never seen a desperate, badass black woman act up."

"What you talking about, missy?"

"I'm talking about what would happen if I oppose you on every front, if I get in your face every time you open your mouth. Whose side they will take if I make it my business to show you up as a lightweight, sissy, wannabe—"

"Hold up! Hold up, Ms. Thing." Vincent hissed, allowing his glasses to slide down the length of his nose before catching it. "You just call me a sissy?"

"Yeah, I called you a sissy," Shantel shot back. "Well, aren't you?"

"Hell no!"

"Well, I just figured. I mean, the way you dress, all retro Boy George. Your whole look. Sometimes your mannerisms."

Vincent burst out laughing. He took off his glasses and wiped his eyes with the back of his hand.

"That's my branding, you ninny," he said, smiling for the first time.

"Your branding?"

"Girlfriend, you cute as hell, but you dumb as a doorknob," he said, sitting back in his seat and replacing his glasses. "As a black man in the advertising business, especially at the creative end, I had to have an image as an eccentric artist type. You think anyone would take me seriously if I came in the building wearing a business suit and carrying a briefcase? I don't think so. Look, all I had was my rep as an uptown graffiti artist and two years at Manhattan College."

Vincent relaxed his angry-black-man, agonizing-artist facade long enough to tell Shantel that he had grown weary of the street hustler life and decided to migrate indoors to the corporate world. He used to be Vince Cadman when he tried on several hats in the advertising business over the last decade. He said he started at the bottom and ran interdepartmental errands at one firm and became assistant to the art director at another. But he remained far behind the leadership horizon for almost a decade. Vincent said that he realized he had to remake himself. He needed a competitive edge over the limitless lines of bright young, recent white college graduates who were willing to work for crumbs.

So he reemerged a few years ago as Vincent Cordeaux, the angry, androgynous, creative but mysteriously brooding genius. He said he and Simone, his girlfriend of seven years, lived in a charming Brooklyn Heights brownstone apartment with a limited view of the East River and Manhattan skyline. Vincent said he was determined to keep the details of his personal life private to intensify the aura of mystery at the agency. But he said he only shared those personal details with Shantel as an act of good faith and in an attempt to solidify their clandestine pact to depose Patsy. In return, Shantel confided in him about her growing ambivalence about motherhood. Once she made that admission, it was easy to share her frustration about the injustice of balancing her career and motherhood.

"I hear you, baby girl," Vincent said, with a hint of compassion that surprised her. He reached across the restaurant table and squeezed her hand affectionately. "I know I'm too damned selfish to be anybody's father. I swear, I wouldn't begin to know how to make time for some damned kids. Shoot, sometimes I feel like there ain't enough time in the day for me to do me."

Shantel knew that she idolized Vincent in that moment. It wasn't a sexual or even an emotional attraction she felt. It was a visceral, magnetic tug. It was as if his millions of tiny selfish atoms suddenly stimulated her countless attention-seeking molecules. The collision of those two connecting magnetic lines of force was almost audible. She knew at that moment that she would entrust her professional career to him. He possessed a striking lack of loyalty and a brashness that she admired. He was parasitic to the extent that he didn't mind poaching and appropriating other people's intellectual property.

Shantel realized then that she envied most of Vincent's personality traits. These were qualities she felt constrained to demonstrate because of family and church expectations. Maybe it was because she was the pastor's daughter, but she fully expected to have the starring role in every Christmas and Easter play. And although she admittedly wasn't blessed with the best singing voice, Shantel could be hostile—even a little vindictive—if the choir director selected someone else to sing a solo. That's why her father always reminded her about the importance of humility.

"God has promised to give grace to the humble, Shantel. He really doesn't like it when you always have to be the center of attention," her father would say.

As a result, he had her memorize and recite 1 Peter 5:5 so often as a child that it became permanently etched in her mind.

> *Therefore, we must confess and put away pride. If we exalt ourselves, we place ourselves in opposition to God who will, in his grace and for our own good, humble us.*

After the coconut water commercial's success, Patsy threw more lucrative accounts at the team. If the other creative team members felt overlooked because Shantel and Vincent assumed leadership of the group, they never expressed it. After all, they already had a generous bonus from one national television commercial under their belts with the promise of more to come. They apparently speculated on the downsides and benefits of working with those two narcissists.

The three of them were obviously satisfied with the established hierarchy. They slugged away for hours, fleshing out concepts from the embryonic stages to various levels of development. And although Shantel and Vincent were often in the bull pen, they rarely contributed significantly. It was clear early on that Terry, Beth and Jeffrey, together or individually, couldn't convincingly pitch a single one of their excellent ideas. It's not that they were inarticulate. They simply lacked the charisma and presence that Shantel and Vincent had acquired over a lifetime in church and on the street. Consequently, with the birth of any new idea, the duo would swoop down, like a couple of eagles on unsuspecting salmon in the stream below. And as soon as they felt they had a few decent leads, they would privately sketch them into a coherent presentation for Patsy. It was a team dynamic that seemed to work for everyone.

But the praise they received from Patsy and the recognition from the agency's partners for being so prolific only added to Shantel and Vincent's craving for more power and control. And they fed into each other's impatience for replacing their creative director.

"Check this out," Shantel said to Vincent one morning in her cubicle before a creative team meeting. "I was doing some rough calculations on the train this morning about the billings our accounts have stacked up for this agency so far."

"Oh yeah?" Vincent responded, rolling his chair closer to her desk. "What'd you come up with?"

"Well, between the coconut water commercial and the four other projects we've worked on, all together we produced about a quarter-million dollars, just in retainer fees alone," Shantel whispered.

She looked intently into Vincent's eyes, reveling in the approval and exhilaration she saw there.

"You know something, little girl?" he whispered, leaning closer in to her. "That's just a drop in the bucket. By the time our ads and commercials go into production, we're looking at a million, maybe two million in billings we'll be responsible for this year."

"I know. I know." Shantel squealed excitedly. "Who knew we'd be so successful so quickly?"

"Hey, missy, pump your brakes," Vincent said gravely, pushing his chair a few inches away from her. "I don't know why you're so excited. It's not as if we getting any of that money. I mean, who gets the bulk of the bonuses?"

"Patsy."

"You got that right. True, she does give us some of the crumbs. But if there's any formal recognition or wining and dining, guess who's getting it?"

"Patsy."

"Right again, girlie!"

"Well, at least the partners know we're the ones who are bussin' our butts to make the campaigns happen."

"That's just it," Vincent said. "They don't know, and they don't care. As far as they're concerned, we don't exist. They know Patsy. They see Patsy. We're just some anonymous widgets on a creative assembly line."

Shantel cupped her chin with one hand as she looked at the sea of administrative assistants banging away at their computer keyboards with robot-like proficiency. They stretched along the entire length of the floor, sandwiched between banks of offices on either side of the space. She couldn't fathom how those women and men could work so diligently in the midst of such anonymity. They were simply bodies attached to computer keyboards. She couldn't do it. She wondered if that was how the agency's partners and account executives considered the creative and production teams—as so many faceless, nameless automatons programmed to produce seductive concepts and perceptions.

"So you're saying that as far as the bosses are concerned," Shantel said, "we don't exist outside of Patsy."

"There you go, girlfriend," Vincent said, rolling up and play-punching her on the arm. "They're only aware of our existence through Patsy. She's, in effect, our eyes, our personalities, and identities to the powers upstairs."

"Well, I guess the question becomes, how do we become Patsy?" Shantel asked.

"I don't believe you went there!" Vincent responded, holding his hands to his mouth in mock surprise. "Uh, uh, uh. Ms. Girl, I taught you well. But you're right. That's exactly it. We have to replace Patsy. You have a problem with that?"

"Who, me? I don't think so," she answered slowly and with emphasis. "I was just thinking that based on the track record we've established for her, Ms. Gay-as-She-Want-to-Be Patsy could now walk into any ad agency up and down Madison Avenue and get hired tomorrow."

"You know you right!" Vincent said.

Suddenly, he propelled his chair toward Shantel and grabbed both of her wrists and squeezed them excitedly.

"Ms. Thing, that's it!"

"What's it? What are you talking about?"

"She's looking for another job."

"Who's looking for another job? Patsy?"

"Yeah, baby girl. Patsy's looking for another job."

"But how'd you know? Who told you?"

"Nobody told me. But that's it. All we have to do is plant the seed."

Vincent's broad smile was infectious. Shantel began smiling also as Vincent's implicit brainstorm seemed to flick across the room with the agility and speed of a hungry tick looking for fresh blood.

The other creative team members had already seated themselves around the conference table when they walked in. As they sat down, Vincent leaned over to Shantel and whispered some gibberish in her ear, loudly enough for Jennifer to hear.

"What?" Shantel responded, genuinely confused.

"That's what I said when I heard it," Vincent said, just above a whisper, but no one around the table missed a word.

"Oh my god," Shantel exclaimed, dramatically covering her mouth with one hand and placing the other over her heart. "Where's she going? To another agency? When? Oh my god!"

The rest of the team members had dropped all efforts of pretending not to eavesdrop by then. They focused intently on Vincent and Shantel, who pretended to ignore them.

By the end of that week, the rumor that Patsy was jumping ship to a larger advertising agency had spread throughout Davidson, Engelman, and Boyd's two floors and beyond. And all week, she remained oblivious to the furtive looks and covert whispers as she frenziedly rushed to her meetings. After all, she managed eight creative teams on the floor. It was the end of business on Friday when Jennifer, her personal assistant, knocked and, without waiting for a response, charged into the office and stood in front of the door, sobbing profusely.

"I just wanted to know when you're actually leaving," Jennifer said between sobs, "and if you planned to take me with you."

"Jennifer, what the hell are you talking about?" Patsy yelled across the room. "Where am I supposed to be going?"

"They say you're going to the Gray Group or to Horizon Media."

"Who's 'they'? And why did 'they' say I'm leaving?"

"I don't know, but everybody's been stopping at my desk since Monday, telling me you're leaving us for a bigger firm. I really thought we had a better relationship than that, Patsy, because it hurt to have to find out from other people on the floor."

"Are you kidding me?" Patsy said, pounding a closed fist on her desk. "I really wish you'd said something to me sooner so I could've nipped this crap in the bud."

But the planted seed had already begun to sprout. The fact that two of New York City's largest ad agencies were interested in Patsy created speculations about her likely successor. In addition, some reliable sources were reporting that the partners were seriously miffed about her decision to bail out so suddenly. They had waited all week on the Twenty-Third Floor for her to come upstairs and formally announce her departure. One persistent rumor on the floor was that Patsy, who had been with the firm from its infancy, was the keeper of many dark secrets. Another rumor had her frustrated for having been passed over repeatedly for a partnership.

The Patsy situation concluded the next Monday morning like the final eruption of a Fourth of July fireworks display. There was anticipation, explosion, and tiny sparks of drizzling light that eventually faded into the darkness. Shantel agonized all weekend that Patsy and the partners would somehow trace the rumor to Vincent and her. Patsy, meanwhile, prepared to go into the partners first thing Monday morning and dispel the rumors that she was leaving the agency. She had prepped herself more thoroughly than she had for any client presentation. She had practiced a convincing argument on why she had no intention of leaving. But the partners, who met briefly Friday evening, made some calls over the weekend to their Madison Avenue counterparts. They concluded by Monday morning that Patsy had started the rumor as a power play for a promotion. They decided unanimously to call her bluff.

Patsy never had the opportunity to make her much-rehearsed presentation to the partners the following Monday morning. They summoned her upstairs, thanked her for her twelve years of loyal and distinguished service to the agency, and wished her well on her future career endeavors. She stepped off the elevator dazed and bewildered to find a crew of maintenance workers wheeling out her filing cabinets, her desk and her cadenza. Patsy walked into her office to find her computer monitor on the floor, surrounded by the few pictures and mementos from her desk. Nothing was strewn around. The maintenance crew left her personal effects in tidy, respectful piles on the floor and sofa. Suddenly, nothing in that once-familiar office seemed to reflect her presence or the thousands of hours she had spent there.

There was a discreet knock on the opened door, and Patsy turned around to see Kathy Kowolski from personnel and a uniformed security guard from the downstairs lobby standing in the hallway. It was as if they had come to escort the body to the morgue.

A woeful stillness blanketed the Twenty-Second Floor as the small procession walked down the center aisle to the elevators. The familiar incessant clicking keyboards ceased, and for a moment, the floor had become deathly silent. Apart from a few unanswered telephones jingling across the gigantic room, the only distinguishable sounds came from the clickety-clack of the security guard's shoes as he led the solemn entourage away.

"So what you think, baby girl?" Vincent whispered into Shantel's ear as they stood together in the bull pen's door, viewing their former boss' departure. "Does Vincent know what he's talking about or what?"

The partners summoned him to a meeting upstairs at nine-thirty the following morning. And for the next twenty minutes, agitated chatter consumed the bull pen. Speculation flew throughout the floor. Although their colleagues had no idea that Shantel and Vincent played any role in Patsy's sudden ejection, they instinctively knew that Vincent's summons upstairs would have an immediate impact on the team. But Shantel refused to be drawn into Terry, Jeffrey and Beth's frenzied speculations. However, she paced impatiently along the room's glass wall, like a caged lioness at the Bronx Zoo. Her emotions alternated between light-headed exhilaration and grave anxiety. She did have the assurance, however, that wherever Vincent went, he would take her with him. But on the other hand, she worried that the partners might have traced the rumor to them. And the longer Vincent remained upstairs, the more Shantel fixated on the latter scenario.

Suddenly, Vincent appeared at the bull pen's door. He pushed it in so hard that the metal handle clanked dangerously against the glass wall. He stood in the doorway expressionless but aware that he was the focus of every pair of eyes in the room. Shantel had to resist the urge to drag him away to some secluded corner to grill him.

"Well, dude," Jeffrey said cheerfully. "You don't seem too battered or bruised, so they must've treated you nicely upstairs."

Vincent didn't respond. He just stood there, slowly and deliberately scanning the faces in the room.

"Oh my god. Oh my god!" Beth yelled. "C'mon, Vincent. You're killing me here. What happened up there?"

Vincent allowed a smile to creep slowly across his face before stepping into the bull pen as the heavy glass door closed behind him.

"Ladies and gentleman," he said, extending his hands in a sweeping gesture of self-introduction. "You're looking at the new creative director of Davidson, Engelman and Boyd."

Because the blinds were open, workers outside the bull pen could see the creative team members jumping and hugging one another. Then they saw Vincent drop into a chair, place his feet on the table, lean back, and lock his fingers behind his head. Every pair of eyes around the conference table strained in his direction. It seemed from the outside that the king was holding court.

The partners, he said, insisted on a seamless transition and wanted Vincent to familiarize himself with the other teams' operations. He told the team they would have to continue the current project without him because he would be conducting an immediate status review of the seven other teams. Shantel was feeling a little uneasy because so far, Vincent hadn't singled her out or made any mention of their partnership in the new arrangement. Her uneasiness grew as she realized he had not looked at her once since he walked into the room. Vincent then told Terry to prepare a status report of the team's current accounts. She was to leave it with Jennifer, his administrative assistant, in his new office first thing in the morning. It was as if he had been exercising this level of authoritative leadership and decisiveness all his life. A queasy anxiety quickly replaced Shantel's initial nervousness. She didn't understand why he was waiting so long to mention her role in the new hierarchy.

Calm down! You should know Vincent by now. He's just messing with you. He's saving the best for last. Watch out now. He's getting ready to tell them you're the assistant creative director or something.

But Vincent abruptly turned and walked toward the door, pulled it opened, and paused.

"Well, it's been real," he said buoyantly. "Toodles. Gotta run. Gotta set up my new office and schedule a bunch of meetings. Got many miles to go, children."

Shantel bolted from the room after Vincent, but he was already surrounded by groups of well-wishers in the hallway, hugging, shaking hands and patting him on the back. It was evident that emails and discreet phone calls had already delivered the news from upstairs. Shantel realized he was effectively insulated from her bitter disappointment and anger by that cocoon of congratulations and admiration. There was no way she could penetrate that outpouring of compliments without appearing like a crazy, envious woman. So she retreated to her cubicle in the middle of the floor and sat at her desk, immobile, for the remainder of the day.

She caught an earlier train home that evening, climbed into bed fully dressed and remained there, staring at the ceiling until darkness erased all traces of form and shadow in the room. The bedside phone rang several times in the blackness, but Shantel had neither the will nor the strength to answer it. Several times, she heard the muffled ringtone of her cell phone buried in her pocketbook somewhere on the floor. But she continued to embrace the darkness and solitude because they shielded her from the intense shame and disenchantment that was trying to consume her.

It's not right! It's just not right! It wasn't supposed to go like this. Didn't I pray for this? Didn't I deserve my own office and staff? Why did I spend all this time praying? I must be praying to the wrong god. When is it going to be my time?

"Shantel! Shantel!"

Shantel awoke to the sound of Rayon shouting her name from downstairs. His shoes, pounding frantically against the hardwood stairs, jolted her awake as he sprinted up to their bedroom. She instinctively looked at the clock radio on the nightstand. Her first thought was that she would miss her train. But as the glowing red LED numbers came into focus, she realized it was 9:45 p.m. She had been sleeping for more than four hours. Rayon burst into the room, turned on the light, and looked down at her. Shantel shielded her eyes from the sudden bright light and turned her head. She heard his breath rushing out of his mouth in short shallow gasps. He had lost so much of his athleticism since college, and she meant to mention how flabby he was becoming, especially in the gut.

"Shants, what's the matter? You OK?

"Yeah, I guess."

"You guess? I was worried sick."

"Why?"

"What do you mean why?" Rayon said, his impatience evident. "My mom called me from my class at seven tonight, very upset because you hadn't picked up Emanuel and she was running late for her Bible study class."

"My god!" Shantel yelled. "Your mother is such a drama queen!"

"She's a drama queen!" Rayon shouted, his voice rising at least one octave. "Well, she's the drama queen that was worried about your sorry behind when you didn't pick up our son. She's the drama queen that kept calling you for almost two hours before she called me. She is the same drama queen who babysits for us every day and has never asked for a dime."

"Don't try to guilt me. That was her own damn choice. Nobody forced her to babysit. That's on her."

"Do you hear yourself? Do you ever listen to the selfish crap that comes out of your mouth sometimes?"

Shantel didn't respond but chose instead to sit up at the edge of the bed and shake her head slowly from side to side. The silence in the room lasted for a few moments as Rayon walked to the window and looked out into the darkness.

"So by the way," he eventually said, much calmer. "Where were you that no one could reach you for hours?"

"Nowhere?" she responded nonchalantly. "I mean here. I was right here."

"Shantel, you got to be kidding me," Rayon replied, his voice rising again. "What the hell kind of mother gets off the train and forgets to pick up her own child whom she hasn't seen all day?"

"Look, I had an unbelievable day," she said, clasping her hands over her head. "I was really stressed out."

"Oh my god!" he shrieked. "Who are you? You must be the mother from hell."

"Don't you judge me, you sanctimonious momma's boy. You have no idea what I have to do to make it out there."

Rayon turned and strode past the bed toward the door before he stopped and looked at Shantel.

"Oh, by the way, in case you come to your senses later and decide to give a damn, the drama queen decided to keep Emanuel tonight because it was late and he was already asleep."

Shantel tried several times the following day to talk with Vincent. But every time she walked over to his office, Jennifer would say he was in a meeting or on an important call. She even asked Jennifer to buzz her the moment Vincent was free, but that buzz never came. Shantel realized she was acting as a pathetic, desperate person. But she reasoned that she had every reason to be desperate. She needed to know her status in the new creative department's hierarchy and to know if Vincent intended to honor any of the promises he made during their conspiracy to get rid of Patsy. She believed she was entitled to at least know where she fit into his vision for the department's future.

The next time she shared space with Vincent was that Thursday morning at an all-hands-on-deck department meeting he called. He sat at one end of the massive conference table while more than thirty account executives, copywriters, and graphic artists wedged themselves around the table. Even Jennifer, his administrative assistant, didn't sit. She stood just behind his right shoulder, notepad and pen at the ready. Vincent was the only one seated, and it was apparent he intentionally staged it like that. He clasped his hands under his chin, tilted his head back, his eyes closed, as if praying.

Shantel knew it was all affect. She knew how he calculated every gesture to heighten the tension and expectation in the room. She had seen him work this heightened drama stich before to seduce potential clients. It was all theater, and everyone in the room had bought tickets to *The Vincent Cordeaux Show*.

He suddenly sat up, strummed the table top rhythmically, as if offering his own introductory drumroll, and stood up. He seemed to survey the faces before him, but Shantel knew he never looked at her. Vincent stepped away from the chair and clasped his hands behind him as he pretended to scan the room, like a general inspecting his troops before battle.

"People," he said, scanning the room again, "it seems as if the gods of faith and chance have suddenly disrupted what was normal and routine for us and decided to rock our world a little bit. It's no secret that Patsy's sudden departure caught us all by surprise."

Shantel saw Jennifer swallow and touch her throat quickly as Vincent mentioned her former boss.

"But the folks upstairs didn't want Madison Avenue to think Patsy's leaving caused us to break our stride," he said. "That's why they didn't advertise a vacancy and decided to replace her immediately from within. You know, they wanted to create a seamless transition. So that's where I came in."

A lone hesitant ripple of applause sounded in the room and ended abruptly as if the applauder thought better of it and abandoned the idea.

"Why, thank you," Vincent said with faux graciousness, placing a hand over his heart and doing a quick courtesy. "At least someone was beginning to think the partners made a good choice."

That brought a smattering of laughter across the conference room.

"But seriously, people, despite what you may think of the bosses' decision to appoint me creative director, they gave us a mandate—although I prefer to see it as an opportunity. Their mandate and our opportunity is to increase our billings by 30 percent by year's end and our production—especially television—by 20 percent."

Vincent allowed the gasps and groans to percolate for a few moments before raising his hand. And like a conductor directing a seasoned symphony orchestra, the buzz instantly dissolved into silence.

"This way, Madison Avenue would realize that Patsy's leaving didn't cripple us. It gave us a boost. Look, everyone in this room is a proven professional. And although our jobs and careers depend on those goals set by the Twenty-Third Floor, our pride and professionalism will make it possible."

Vincent's casual mention that their professional lives hung in the balance created a fresh and prolonged wave of muttering. But since he had decided earlier that the event would be a monologue, he didn't entertain any dialogue with his audience.

"So I don't know about you, but I'm not prepared to fail," he said zealously. "We are going to prepare ourselves for the task. That's because it's all about preparation in this business. We are going to prepare our asses off as if our lives depend on it."

Shantel studied the faces around her and was surprised by how quickly and completely her colleagues were buying what Vincent was selling.

So all of a sudden, he's a life coach and a motivational speaker. What a load of crap.

"I think it was Samuel Taylor Coleridge who said, 'He who is best prepared can best serve his moment of inspiration.' People, this is our moment of inspiration, and we are prepared for whatever challenges come from upstairs."

This time, the applause was spontaneous and resounding.

"Thank you. Thank you," Vincent said. He smiled broadly and raised his hands for silence. "I have one more announcement."

As the room fell silent, Vincent scanned the faces until he found Shantel's. He seemed to smile at her.

"In anticipation of our increased productivity, the partners upstairs have authorized me to hire an assistant creative director."

Finally! That man is such a drama queen. He really got me this time. Whew! He really had me going there for a while. I don't know why he had to drag it out like this. Must be a power thing. It's always a power trip with Vincent. Well, better late than never.

"People," Vincent said, still smiling. "Allow me to introduce our new assistant creative director, Mr. Simon Howard."

What the hell just happened? What the hell is this?

Shantel felt a sudden, intensely sharp pain zip across her temples. Her mouth became instantly dry, and she found it impossible to pry her lips apart. She hadn't realized her legs had given out beneath her until one of the men standing next to her began helping her to a chair. He smelled faintly like the lilac flowers her mother placed in their dining room in the spring—refreshing and reassuring.

"Simon, come over here," Vincent said cheerfully, beckoning to the balding, little man leaning over Shantel at the back of the room.

Simon Howard straightened up, smiled, and walked toward Vincent. He was slender but far from frail. A close-cropped salt-and-pepper beard created a hint of mannishness that seemed to be at odds with his meticulously manicured nails and fastidious fashion sense. He wore a soft-beige silk shirt and maroon bowtie under a tight-fitting double-breasted blue silk blazer. The cuffs of his impeccably creased white slacks flawlessly covered the laces of his blue-and-white wing-tipped shoes. He stood close to Vincent with a casualness that betrayed some level of familiarity between them.

"Simon is no stranger to our business," Vincent began, putting his hand on the smaller man's shoulder and patting it gently. "You've probably seen his work all over the place. That's because he has managed several accounts in the fragrance and cosmetics industry over the years. Simon has worked on some of the huge campaigns for industry giants such as Max Factor, Chanel, and Revlon. He's a dear friend, and I know I imposed on that friendship to get him to temporarily give up his retirement to work here with us. Let me tell you, it was the hardest pitch I've ever had to make."

After some polite chuckles and the certainty that Simon was not going to speak, the room emptied quickly as people drifted off in groups to process the rapid succession of events. By the time Vincent walked into his office, Shantel was already seated on his sofa. He didn't see her until he sat behind his desk and was reaching for his phone. He was clearly more annoyed than shocked to see her.

"How'd you get in here?" he barked.

"Your pit bull is obviously not on the job," Shantel shot back. "She's too busy spreading your lies out there."

"OK, you had your say. Now, is there anything else I can do for you?"

"Yeah. You can begin by telling me why you screwed me over so royally."

"Oh, that's easy. It's what I do," Vincent said nonchalantly. "Ever heard the story of the fox that gave the scorpion a ride on his back across a river? I'm sure you heard it. As the fox was swimming to the other side, the scorpion suddenly stung him. And with his dying breath, the fox asked, 'Why'd you sting me?' And the scorpion replied, 'It's what I do.'"

"You are stone, cold and heartless. You know that?" Shantel said, close to tears. "We made plans. I trusted you."

"See, little girl," he said, ruffling through some papers on his desk. "That's your problem right there. You trusted me, but I never trusted you."

"Oh my god, Vincent. That's cold," she moaned. "I had your back the whole time. You could've at least thrown me a bone. You could've let me come in as your assistant."

"Nah," he said, still moving piles of folders around on his desk. "That wouldn't have worked for me."

"But why not? We started this thing together."

"Well, girlie-girl, with you as my assistant, I would be too distracted wondering how you planned to take me out. Plus, my partner needed a job."

Shantel felt the dizziness again. Only this time, she was already seated.

"What partner?" She gasped, patting her chest. "Simon?"

Vincent nodded his head.

"But you told me your partner was a woman. You told me her name was Simone. Oh my god, you told me y'all lived in Brooklyn."

"What can I say? I lied. Well, I take that back. I only lied about the name. Simone is really Simon, and we've been together for years."

"But you told me you were straight and the gay stuff was just you fronting to confuse the white folk."

"Sweetie, I'm as gay as a jaybird, and I've been gay all my life," Vincent said, finally focusing his attention on Shantel. "Your problem was that you were so blinded by your own greed, you refused to see the real deal. You're too weak and blind to be a leader. And frankly, you'd be a liability."

Shantel was bawling uncontrollably by then. Her gut-wrenching howls could be heard beyond the office. Jennifer stepped inside the door in wide-eyed panic, but Vincent waved her away. After she closed the door behind her, Vincent continued to observe Shantel with the detachment of a kitten eyeing a discarded toy.

After a few minutes, when her shrill wailing subsided to muted gasps, Vincent pushed back his chair and stood up as a signal of dismissal. Shantel was a picture of defeat and humiliation as she lifted herself from the sofa. Her eyes were red and puffy; her makeup and tears created macabre, garish streams that trickled down her cheeks and chin and descended down her long slender neck and into her bosom.

"Oh, by the way, you remember that bone you wanted me to throw you?" Vincent said. "Well, I have one for you. You could say, for old times' sake."

He said the agency recently learned that United Airlines intended to buy US Airways by mid to late 2000. But before United swallowed US Airways, officials wanted to project the image of a bigger, stronger, but more compassionate air carrier. They were shopping around for an advertising agency with the agility to crank out a powerful campaign to project a large but caring airline by the time the merger took place. The expected roll out date was in six months.

The turnaround was much too tight for most of their larger competitors, but according to Vincent, the partners believed the agency was nimble and edgy enough to pull it off. Vincent said his strategy was to create some internal competition among the eight creative teams. The teams that came in with the two most impressive concepts would be assigned to merge and develop a presentation that he and Simon would eventually pitch to United in Chicago.

"That'll be a mega account, girlie," Vincent said enthusiastically. "If we land this, I can see us moving a team out to Chicago just to service that account. You feelin' me?"

Shantel felt herself suddenly and inexorably transported again to that familiar place of ambitious exhilaration. She could see herself moving from

New York to head up the agency's Chicago office. Such a move would more than make up for the humiliation and betrayal she had been forced to endure.

"So what do I have to do, Vincent?"

"Look," he whispered furtively, although they were alone in the office. "I'm giving you the rest of today and all weekend as a head start to come up with three or four dynamic concepts and at least twenty taglines."

"That's a lot of work, man," Shantel protested. "How am I expected to come up with three entire concepts and all those taglines by Monday?"

"See, there you go," he said, with a trace of exasperation. "It's that same lack of initiative and leadership that will keep you running with the herd all your life."

"C'mon, man," she responded. "Be honest. You're setting me up to fail again, aren't you? You know that's an unreasonable expectation for me to complete a full week's work, at the very least, in one weekend."

"You still don't get it," Vincent said, shaking his head slowly. "You asked for a bone, and I threw you a bone. But now you're complaining that the bone's too hard. You really are not a leader. You know what you are? You're a whiney little complainer. You see, leaders don't complain about problems. Leaders solve problems."

"I'm sorry," she said. "I'm just so stressed out right now."

"Look, if I were you and somebody gave me a heads-up this huge, I would pull my team together immediately. I would take charge. Then I'd tell them what's at stake and demand they come in early Saturday morning. I'd tell them to be prepared to work through the weekend if necessary because this is big. It could be a game changer. But that's just me. You have the bone. Now let me see what you do with it."

Vincent nudged her out of the office and shut the door. Minutes later, the team members couldn't hide their excitement about the possibility of working on the United Airlines campaign. Jeffrey and Terry immediately agreed to come in to work on Saturday and Sunday, if necessary. Beth, however, had plans with her family for Saturday but would skip church on Sunday. Shantel's exhilaration was peaking again. She allowed herself to feel a little of the rush she expected to experience when she landed the account. She expected to feel the actual elation when she became head copywriter for the project. But she knew her moment of euphoria would come when the agency transferred her to head up the new Chicago office.

Shantel was in great spirits on the ride home. She spent most of the ride mapping out her career trajectory after winning the United Airlines account and moving to Chicago. By the time the train stopped in Beacon, she was the founder and CEO of her own advertising and marketing agency, with offices in New York, London, and Tokyo. She was in an enchanted place and knew the feeling would fizzle away once she walked through her front door. So instead of making the five-minute drive from the train station to the condo, Shantel decided to drive over the mile-long Newburgh-Beacon Bridge to Newburgh. She would treat herself to her favorite pizza for dinner. Rayon, she knew, wasn't a pizza fan, but he would tolerate a slice or two from Bernie's Gourmet Pizza if he had to. She called ahead and ordered a medium shrimp, Cajun chicken, and broccoli pie.

They ate dinner, mostly in silence, except for a few perfunctory comments about the Friday evening crowds in Grand Central and about Emanuel's new teeth. Rayon mentioned that his mother pointed out a slight rash on the baby's cheek when he picked Emanuel up earlier. Conversations between them recently, even the most banal discussions, had become notably labored.

"Mom said we shouldn't be concerned," he said. "She said it's pretty common with babies, especially in the summer."

"Uh-huh."

A few minutes later, as Rayon was clearing off the dinner table, Shantel called out to him from the kitchen.

"Hey, before I forget, you gotta watch Emanuel tomorrow."

"Why is that?"

"Well, I have to go into the office for a while."

"What's *a while*?"

"A couple of hours, and maybe on Sunday also."

"Uh-uh," Rayon said, walking into the kitchen. "That's not happening!"

"What do you mean it's not happening?" Shantel responded, her voice shrilly and nasal. "This is important. This is work."

"I don't care. You're not running off to Manhattan all weekend. You have a child here at home, for Christ's sake. You have responsibilities here."

"But this is important. This is a major ..."

"I don't care! You just don't come in here, out of the blue, and announce you're going to work all weekend and everything simply stops for you."

"What if it was you going off to preach for the whole weekend at God knows where? Everything would stop for you, wouldn't it?"

"The difference is, I'd be more considerate. I wouldn't pop it on you at the last minute. I've always told you that in my life, it's God first, family second and ministry third. Next to God, my family's the most important thing to me. So no. I wouldn't take a preaching assignment at the last minute and leave my family high and dry."

"Yeah, Ray, that sounds real nice and noble and all that. But this is a big opportunity for me. This could be a huge career boost for me, and I'm not gonna let you blow it for me. This is not about family. You understand what I'm saying? This is not about church. You hear me? This is not about anybody but me. *Me!*"

"Oh my god!" Rayon screamed. "I doubt God ever made a more selfish creature than you."

He was tempted to slam the front door shut as he stalked out of the condo, but he had just put Emanuel to sleep thirty minutes earlier. Instead, he pulled it gently behind him until he heard the latch click. Rayon fought the urge to call his mother. She had always been his sounding board whenever he needed to vent. She had this remarkable gift of listening without interjection or judgment. But he remembered the Hills and the Hendricks left Thursday morning to attend a church convention in Douglasville, Georgia. Then they planned to rent a car and drive to Pompano Beach, Florida, after the convention to look at some adjoining retirement properties.

It's not like she didn't know I have plans for tomorrow. She knows I have to be somewhere.

Rayon made time to play golf with a few of his pastor colleagues at least once a month at McCann's—a public golf course in Poughkeepsie. He wasn't a good golfer. Actually, he didn't like the sport. But he cherished the camaraderie and the chance to share ministry horrors and highpoints only pastors can appreciate.

So Shantel had to devise a plan. She was up and dressed by seven on Saturday. Then she dressed and fed Emanuel by seven forty-five. She then drove to the Metro-North station to catch the 8:08 that would get her to Grand Central by nine forty-five. Once on the train, she wedged Emanuel's car seat next to the window, propped a bottle of apple juice between his lips, and encouraged him to wrap his pudgy little baby fingers around the plastic feeding bottle. He was asleep before they got to Garrison, two stops down.

But Shantel had already pulled out her laptop as the train rolled out of the Beacon station. If she were to assume leadership of the team, she'd better have a road map at least. She tapped away purposefully on the keyboard. She was determined to walk into the bull pen with at least a dozen taglines to show her colleagues she had taken some leadership initiative.

- United Airlines, bigger and better.
- United Airlines, determined to get you there faster, safer.
- At United Airlines, we're bigger but friendlier.
- More planes, more people to get you to your destination faster—United.
- United Airlines. More seats, more experience. Fly United.

The taglines came slowly and laboriously at first. But after a while, Shantel hit her stride, and the ideas flew to the keyboard with the intensity of hailstones slamming against a metal screen door.

Shantel left Grand Central Station through the Lexington Avenue exit and raced up the avenue. There wasn't the usual jostling and maneuvering through the throngs on the sidewalk because it was relatively early on Saturday morning. But she couldn't shut off the tapes that were playing in her head as she trooped up the avenue to the office.

Fly the friendly skies of . . . No, no, no, no. That's been done. C'mon. C'mon. I know, how about "Trust us, we'll always get you there.—United." "Let us get you there. United Airlines is committed to getting you there." "More planes, more people" . . . No, no, we already did that. "At United Airlines, we'll do whatever it takes to keep you coming back."

By the time Shantel walked into the bull pen, Jeffrey and Terry were already seated at the conference table, sipping coffee and reading through stacks of each other's flash cards. She immediately plugged her computer into the projector and beamed her taglines to a pull-up screen across the room. It never occurred to her to even consider Jeffrey's and Terry's ideas until she had run through her exhaustive list. Without Vincent's presence and influence to decisively shoot down wispy ideas, they soon generated more tension than consensus. The spirited wrangling over a workable concept for the United Airlines project continued nonstop for more than two hours until Terry suggested a lunch break. But Shantel still had not been able to grasp the leadership reigns from the team all morning. However, she still had the remainder of the day. She would start jockeying for that position right after lunch.

Then it hit her. Emanuel must be past hungry by now. She hadn't had time to feed him after they left home this morning. All he had was that bottle of apple juice since then.

Why isn't he crying? He should be crying up a storm by now. Lord knows that child loves to eat. Where'd I set him down?

Shantel hastily glanced around the room before rising from her chair to look into the empty chairs around the glass-topped conference table.

"Oh my god!" she wailed into her opened hands.

"Is something wrong?" Terry asked.

"Oh my god!" Shantel cried out again. "Where's Emanuel?"

"Where's who?" Jeffrey asked, clearly puzzled and slowly lifting himself from his chair. "Who is Emanuel?"

"That's her son," Terry answered softly.

Shantel began frantically pulling out chairs from around the table.

"Shantel." Jeffrey took a hesitant step toward her. "Why are you looking for your son in here?"

"I don't know. I don't know where he is," Shantel moaned.

"Maybe you left him in your cubicle," Terry suggested.

"No. I came right in here this morning. I didn't go anywhere else. Oh my god."

"Was he in anything?" Jeffrey asked. "Were you carrying him in your arms?"

"No. I mean, um, yes. I was carrying him in his little car seat thing . . ."

"Did you drive in?" Terry asked. "Maybe he's in the car."

Shantel gasped then froze. She looked at her colleagues with sad, defeated eyes before a veil of intense fear crept across her face. It was as if she had come to some dreadful realization that she was standing alone in the path of a river of molten lava. She looked inextricably defeated.

"Oh god! Oh god! Oh god!" she moaned and ran out of the room toward the elevators.

Shantel bolted down Lexington Avenue and ducked into the first Grand Central Terminal entrance. She leaned against a wall to catch her breath and to compose herself.

It mightn't be as bad as it looks. Maybe somebody already brought Emanuel to the lost and found or to the missing babies or whatever. I'm sure people forget their kids all the time. I'll bet they have him waiting for me to pick him up. They better not try to yell at me or try to lecture me because I'm not trying to hear all that yang yang. People don't understand. I have a very high-pressure job.

She managed to remain calm and breezy when she asked a pair of Metropolitan Transit Authority officers for directions to the lost and found office. Her confidence increased with every step.

After all, if someone found a baby on the train, the logical thing to do would be to turn the child over to an MTA cop. I mean, that's what I would do. Who wouldn't? Really. Who would want to take on the responsibility of some kid they never saw before? I know I sure wouldn't!

Shantel became the focus of intense attention moments after walking into MTA's police offices. She was forced to repeat her story to a civilian woman at the reception desk twice. The receptionist quickly disappeared briefly, only to return with a disheveled burly black detective and a middle-aged woman who displayed the parched lips and lined face of a heavy smoker. They led her into a small office with two facing gray steel desks along one wall. A battery of gray metal filing cabinets occupied every inch along the remaining walls. A pair of green-and-gray metal chairs stood at the exposed end of each desk. The room smelled of musty cigarette smoke and felt as somber and foreboding as its occupants.

The woman waved Shantel to a chair and dropped into the wooden swivel chair behind the desk. The chair was obviously a relic from an earlier era. The brass nameplate on the desk said, "Det. Halina Novinsky." Her partner pushed some files out of the way, sat down on his desk, and plopped his feet onto his swivel chair. His nameplate announced, "Det. Horatio Pittman." Novinsky fished a pen out of a jar on her desk and tapped it on a notepad in front of her several times, as if she were counting down a tune.

"Now, lemme get this straight," she said finally, her voice as craggy as a crow's. "You forgot your kid on the train and went off to work?"

Shantel turned to look at Pittman, hoping their shared ethnicity would elicit some compassion. But seeing the same incredulous look, she returned her attention to the woman.

"Well, yes," Shantel began. "But it's not as bad as it sounds."

"This I gotta hear," Pittman said.

"Y'all have to understand," Shantel said, looking from one detective to the other. "I'm under a lotta stress on my job. It's unbelievable how much pressure I'm dealing with."

"This is getting good," Novinsky said solemnly, leaning into Shantel with exaggerated fascination. "You have a high-powered job with so much stress that you leave your kid on the train. What are you, the mayor of New York City, under such pressure? What do you do anyway?"

"I'm a copywriter for an ad agency," she responded brightly. "You have no idea how creatively demanding it is out there."

"Let me see if I'm getting this," Pittman said. "Your very important, very high-stress job is to come up with crap like 'Where's the beef?'"

"Oh, oh, I got one," Novinsky said, exposing a hint of a smile. "'Double your pleasure, double your fun.' And something about buying Doublemint gum. Is that the kind of deep, creative zingers that made you abandon your kid on the train for hours and hours?"

"Y'all just don't get it," Shantel protested. "It's super competitive on Madison Avenue. The constant pressure of coming up with convincing, creative ideas takes over your life."

"Is that so?" Pittman said, angrily pushing his chair across the room until it crashed noisily against a filing cabinet. "If I lost a child of mine every time I had some stress here, I would've run out of children my first week on the job. So save that BS for someone who don't know better."

"You're just being unnecessarily mean," Shantel said.

"So I want you to help me understand how it is that you got off the train, went to work for—what, three, four hours?" Novinsky asked. "And never once missed your baby. Can you help me understand how that could happen?"

"Look," Shantel shot back, "all I want to know is, did someone find Emanuel? Did someone pick him up and bring him in? I just want to get my son and go home. OK?"

"But you see, that's just the thing," Novinsky said. "Nobody's brought your kid in. We're just trying to figure out why you would abandon your kid on the train."

"Abandon?" Shantel screeched. "Abandon? Why would you say that? Why would I abandon my child?"

"I don't know," Pittman interjected. "What would you call it? You left your son and walked off the train in the middle of New York City. Who does that?"

"So yes, Ms. . . ." Detective Novinsky glanced down at the police report on her desk briefly. "Ms. Hendricks, is it? We're talking about abandonment for starters."

"I don't believe this," Shantel said, burying her face in her hands. "I need to talk to my husband. Y'all need to let me call my husband."

Because she had left her pocketbook with her phone in the bull pen, the detectives allowed her to use one of the office phones. Rayon's cell phone rang several times before it went to voice mail. She remembered that he and his golf buddies never took their phones out on the course. Shantel left Rayon Detective Pittman's phone number before leaving a similar message on their house phone. The detectives then left her in the office for a ten-minute meeting with their lieutenant.

Later, they told Shantel they decided to publicize Emanuel's disappearance in the hope that someone might have seen the baby. Every moment counted, they insisted. They said their communications people needed a picture of the child. So two uniformed officers escorted her to the building, and a security guard accompanied them to the deserted conference room to retrieve her pocketbook. They were able to find one usable photo of Emanuel on her phone.

Later that afternoon as Rayon drove back to Beacon from Poughkeepsie, he felt an irrepressible urge to play with his son. He hadn't seen Emanuel since he gave him a bath and put him to bed the night before. He would get a haircut, pick up some barbequed chicken for dinner, and take Emanuel out in his stroller. Rayon felt a pang of joyful anticipation about seeing his son. He anticipated the broad smile and the miniature emerging front teeth when he scooped Emanuel up and held him over his head before swinging him down. Rayon could never get enough of his baby's joyful gurgles. He imagined that Shantel should be already home as he approached the Beacon exit off I-84.

He had just found a parking spot on Main Street and was a few steps from the barbershop when his cell phone rang. It was Cherrylin Buckman, his administrative assistant. She was efficient and thorough, as long as she didn't have to make decisions. Cherrylin had to be the most responsibility-averse person he had ever known. But it was unusual for her to call him on Saturday unless she needed direction on some major crisis, such as whether to include the church's fall revival in this Sunday's bulletin.

"Hi, Cherrylin," Rayon said breezily. "Who died?"

"Pastor, you seen the news?" Cherrylin said, her voice pitched and anxious.

"What news?" he responded, his hand on the barbershop's door handle. "What's going on?"

Rayon released the door as feelings of anxiety and alarm overwhelmed him.

"Pastor, is about the baby," she said hesitantly and filled with emotion. "Is about Emanuel."

"What? What about Emanuel?"

"Is all over the news. They saying they can't find him..."

"What you mean they can't find him? He's with his mother. He's with Shantel."

It didn't make sense. The anxiety he felt moments earlier intensified. His temples throbbed like the rhythm section of a Latin band. He heard Cherrylin's voice squawking as if she had been calling to him from a foggy distance. It felt eerie and dreamlike before he realized he had dropped the phone to the sidewalk. Miraculously, it remained intact. A few men trickled out from the barbershop and instinctively formed a tight, silent circle around Rayon. They had seen the story a few minutes earlier and were in the middle of a somber discussion about the lost baby when someone pointed to Rayon outside on the sidewalk.

It was already dark when Rayon sprinted across Forty-Second Street and dashed into the bowels of Grand Central Station. Earlier, two men from the barbershop insisted they would drive him to Manhattan despite his feeble protests. He sat on the back seat of the SUV, mostly silent, except to respond to the men's repeated inquiries about how he was doing. Rayon didn't remember much else about the trip because his mind raced with hundreds of unanswered questions. Images of Emanuel, lost and terrified, played constantly in his head, like out-of-control black-and-white newsreels.

After a brief conversation of incomprehensible statements by blurred, faceless individuals in a reception area, a woman led Rayon down what felt like an interminably long corridor. She stopped at a green metal door, knocked briefly, opened the door, and gestured him in. As the door swung open, Rayon saw Shantel seated behind a large metal table that appeared to take up most of the room. Her hands cupped her face as she slouched over the table. Her eyes were closed as if in a deep sleep. A woman with strands of stringy, unkempt black-and-white hair sat at one end of the table. She turned to look at him. A burly, black man stood at the other end of the table with one foot planted in a chair.

Rayon burst into the room and stomped over to Shantel.

"Shantel!" he bellowed.

She jerked erect in the chair, stunned and disoriented.

"Shantel!" Rayon hollered again, this time leaning forward to within inches from her face. "Where's Emanuel? Where is my son?"

She dropped her head into a crocked arm on the table.

Rayon grabbed a handful of hair and yanked her head back. Her long slender neck curved backward, the terror in her eyes unmistakable. Detective Novinsky did not react, but her partner took his foot off the chair and stood up. Neither of them attempted to intercede.

"Shantel, I asked you," Rayon said slowly, between his teeth, almost whispering, his voice frosty and menacing. "Where is my son?"

"Oh god, Rayon." She sobbed. "I don't know. I don't know."

"You don't know?" he responded, tugging her head further back. Her neck was now a fluid arc. "Is that what you're telling me? You don't know what you did with my son?"

The detectives were on either side of Rayon by then, attempting to free Shantel's hair from his hand and to move him away. But he swung his free hand in a swift, forceful arc toward her neck. The impact made a ghastly sound. There was a horrendous crack, as if some unseen audience had clapped their hands once in unison. Rayon shook himself free from the stunned detectives and shoved Shantel's head toward the table with extraordinary force. They watched in stunned silence as her head smashed onto the steel-topped table, the perfect arc of Shantel's neck now distorted and angular. She looked blankly across the room, the shock of death clearly registered on her face.

Rayon remained indifferent to everything around him during the months after Shantel's death. He languished in jail for nine months, awaiting trial on charges of murder in the second degree. And during that time, as he was shuttled to court for several preliminary hearings, Rayon remained apathetic about the proceedings and indifferent to the urgings of his attorneys to participate in his own defense.

He rejected attempts by relatives and colleagues to appeal to his faith in God to see him through the legal catastrophe. And especially shocking—particularly to his parents—was his flat rejection of any suggestions to pray with them. Their visits to Rikers Island eventually ceased when it became clear that Rayon refused to participate in any conversations that included Christianity or any references to God. It was obvious that he had shut that door when he removed from his visitors' list everyone who persisted in raising those topics.

But Rayon actually began closing that door during the ride to Grand Central Station in the SUV. He had already determined that if they found Emanuel, he would have something to say to and about God. But if it turned out that he would never hold his baby son in his arms again, then nothing mattered. His life, his wife, his ministry and his parents would become valueless to him. If the God for whom he sacrificed his music did not see fit to restore his son to him, then he would no longer serve him.

As he rode to Manhattan in the darkness of the car, Rayon thought of Abraham on the verge of sacrificing his son Isaac. He tried to envision Abraham's mind-set as he prepared to plunge the dagger into his son's heart. Rayon tried to embrace some portion of the faith it must have taken for that loving father to even begin building a sacrificial altar with only his son Isaac in sight. Was Abraham's dogged obedience based only on God's earlier promise to make him the father of a great nation? He couldn't comprehend how any father could wrap his fingers around a dagger intended for sacrifice as his innocent son reclined in perfect trust on that altar of death.

Those passages in Genesis 22:11 and 12 came to Rayon with perfect clarity as he closed his eyes while the car barreled down the winding Taconic Parkway.

> But the angel of the LORD called out to him from heaven, "Abraham! Abraham!" "Here I am," he replied. "Do not lay a hand on the boy," he said. "Do not do anything to him. Now I know that you fear God, because you have not withheld from me your son, your only son."

Rayon believed that God had divinely placed a ram in the thicket as a replacement for Isaac's life. He also believed that Abraham's unquestioning faith in God resulted in the father and son walking down from Mount Moriah unharmed.

Well, that worked out for Abraham. What about your own faith? How much do you trust God? Do you have the faith that you and Emanuel will walk down from Mount Moriah together?

Lying back in the SUV, Rayon tried to conjure up some measure of that Abrahamic faith. A bereaved mother once asked him if her eight-year-old daughter would have survived lymphoma if she and her husband had exercised more faith and prayed harder. He recalled giving her a convoluted answer that in retrospect must have left her more bewildered. He just never had a firm personal grasp on the whole *faith* issue. Rayon closed his eyes and tried to create an image of a smiling, reassuring God in whom he had complete faith. But it was like trying to flex muscles that had long since deteriorated into atrophy. The personal God that he once knew had become a mystical acquaintance to whom he occasionally offered perfunctory praises and public prayer.

He had reluctantly risen through the ranks to become a preacher, pastor and now a bishop because of his preacher's pedigree. His father's ministry connections had enabled him to preach from several prestigious pulpits across the country. Rayon recognized he had become an excellent pulpit performer. But he would unquestionably have preferred his performances to have been on a jazz stage.

And as the SUV approached New York City, Rayon realized he had no authentic testimony of faith, no repertoire of personal accomplishments of belief from which he could draw. He acknowledged that God had no reason to honor any of his prayers. So rather than approach God as a crisis Christian, Rayon decided instead, to broker an agreement.

I know I haven't been one hundred percent with you. I've been distracted and preoccupied with the roles I've had to play as some kind of caring, compassionate pastor. It's not like you didn't know from the beginning that my heart wasn't in it. But for some reason, you never give me a way out. It was always about what my parents wanted. It's what my father lived for—my becoming a bishop one day and taking over his churches. But where's my thing? They say you know our thoughts and our plans even before we were born. So don't you think you kinda owe me a little bit for the time I put in serving your people? Well, anyway, here's the thing. If you give me back my baby, I swear I will do whatever you want me to. I will go wherever you send me. If you restore my son back to me, I will serve you and worship you in spirit and in truth until I die. For real! But if you don't return my son to me, we're done.

By the time Rayon walked into the interrogating room that night, he knew he shouldn't have attempted to make deals with God. He knew he must have crossed the line because of a foreboding heaviness he felt in his spirit. The certainty that he would never see his son again began to press down on him, like a powerful hand forcing him down into a lake of dark, murky water. His attack on Shantel resulted from the deep conviction that

Emanuel was already dead. That conviction produced in him a hot, white anger that burned against God and his instrument of death, Shantel.

Although he was charged with second-degree murder, Rayon's lawyers, Rita Washington and Ronald Wayne of Jonathan Greenblatt Law Offices, New Windsor, initially thought they had a decent chance of acquittal if they went for an extreme emotional disturbance defense. However, to pull that off, Rayon would have to play a major role in his own defense. He would have to testify about the sudden shock and anguish he experienced when he learned of his only child's disappearance. He would have to convince a jury that he had no plan or intention of killing his wife before entering the interview room. The jury would have to believe that his striking out at Shantel was an involuntary action precipitated by intense grief. But it soon became clear to Rayon's attorneys that any defense that relied so heavily on their client's participation would be futile. He remained uncooperative and sometimes hostile when they met. And in addition, he refused to comply with even the most fundamental requests for collaboration.

"I don't understand why you guys insist on wasting your time," Rayon said during one of the initial meetings at Rikers Island. "Although, I do have nothing but time. But the way I see it, nothing we say or do will bring back my son. I know my daddy's paying you to do what you do. But you'll have to do it without me. Y'all trying to get me out, right? Well, what if I told you I don't want to get out? Frankly, there's nothing for me out there anymore."

His lawyers met later with Andrea Lopez, an assistant district attorney from the Manhattan DA's office, hoping to have the charges reduced at least to involuntary manslaughter. They argued that Rayon killed his wife in the heat of passion and that he did not have enough time to collect his thoughts and feelings after learning of his son's disappearance and possible death.

"He was a distraught father who acted in the heat of passion," Wayne said. "He didn't step into that room with the intent to murder his wife."

"Nice try," Lopez said. "But we're sticking with second-degree murder. Your client's looking at a solid fifteen to twenty-five years."

"But why?" Washington interjected. "C'mon. Do you really believe this rises to the level of depraved disregard? We're not talking about a pattern of spousal abuse here or about someone who planned to murder his wife. This is a man of God here, a bishop who lost it for a moment under tragic circumstances."

Lopez, a petite woman who looked deceptively youthful, had a reputation as a tough prosecutor. The New Windsor lawyers were briefed that her combative style was probably overcompensation for her diminutive stature. She stood at the head of her office's small conference table while the defense lawyers sat and were forced to look up at her.

"Look, the only reason we're having this conversation is as a courtesy," the assistant DA said. "My boss knows your boss from somewhere. But I'm not here to do you any favors. You're lucky I'm not going for felony murder. That's life without parole for your guy."

"Aw, now that's excessive, Ms. Lopez. Very extreme," Wayne said, his voice shrill and rising. "You'd have to prove that our client came to the scene with the intent to kill his wife."

"You're damn right," Lopez responded. "And don't think for a moment I couldn't prove it. But I'm in a compassionate mood, so I'm sticking with the second-degree charge. And just for the record, I couldn't care less if your client is a bishop or the pope. I'm taking him down."

"Look, Ms. Lopez," Washington said, rising from her chair and towering above the assistant DA. "I know you have a job to do just as we have a job to do. But what's really going on here? Why the hard line?"

"Well, for one thing," Lopez answered, "your client had lots of time to plan his wife's murder as he drove into Manhattan. I'll say he had about an hour, and that's enough time to work out a plan to murder. The other thing is, I've seen your client. He doesn't show the slightest remorse. He looks way too cold-blooded."

"Those your only reasons?" Wayne asked sarcastically as he stood up. "Or is this all about the media circus surrounding this case? Don't think that because we're Upstate that we don't see the news. 'Bishop Kills Wife in Police Station' or 'Woman Slain After Leaving Baby on Train.' This is a big case, and everybody's watching. We all know you plan on making your bones with this case."

The case played out pretty much as ADA Lopez had predicted. The prosecution presented a convincing picture of an angry, volatile, and demanding husband who resented his wife's professional success. But there was little hope of any rebuttal because Rayon vehemently refused to take the stand to testify in his own defense.

"Look, I don't know how else to tell you guys," he told Washington and Wayne. "I appreciate what you're trying to do here. But I'm not trying to get acquitted. I'm not trying to get a reduced sentence. I'm not trying to walk out of here and go home. I have no home to go back to. I have nobody to go back to. Just get it over with already."

"Bishop Hendricks ..." Washington began, but Rayon cut her off.

"Please stop calling me Bishop," he said. "You know how ridiculous that sounds to me?"

"OK, OK, Mr. Hendricks. Rayon," Washington continued. "Your father is paying us good money to defend you. And win or lose, we're still getting paid. But we want to feel like we're earning our pay here. You've got to help us help you."

Rayon shrugged, leaned back in his chair, and fixed his gaze on the ceiling fan whirling noiselessly above the bench. They heard the faint jingle of his foot chains as he shifted his feet.

He sat at the defense table every day in the same wrinkled suit, unshaven and stoic. He was emphatic about not wanting his parents, his congregation, or anyone he knew in the courtroom. And he bluntly rejected all offers of help from people he knew. But his defense team insisted on his wearing the suit that they bought him from a JCPenney in a Paramus, New Jersey mall. Still, they tried repeatedly but unsuccessfully to get his parents and church members to testify about his temperament and disposition. Rayon, however, was adamant about not having anyone testify in his defense. And although the prosecution could find no witnesses to attest to any history of abuse or violence, ADA Lopez persistently portrayed Rayon as dangerously explosive. So she played up the MTA detectives' testimony of their brief but fatal encounter with Rayon. Theirs was the only evidence of his temperament the jury heard.

Compounding the jury's guilty verdict was the judge's castigation of Rayon for his lack of remorse and his apparent indifference about his wife's death throughout the trial. He made it clear later at the sentencing trial that Washington and Wayne should expect no leniency for their client. The judge said he was repulsed by Rayon's indifference to everything and everyone during the three-week trial.

"You, sir, are a disgrace to clergypersons everywhere," he said. "I'm disgusted by your callous disregard for the life you took. You have not demonstrated any concern for the feelings of your late wife's parents or for everyone who loved her. You even declined an opportunity to apologize to the victim's parents. Very seldom do I see defendants pass up an opportunity to make themselves seem more humane. But you, sir, you just didn't care. So because you have shown yourself to be the cold-hearted killer that you are, I will exercise every bit of authority invested in me by the great state of New York. I will ensure your confinement to the fullest extent of the law."

As he heard the fifteen- to twenty-five-year sentence, Rayon left the judge flabbergasted when he displayed an almost imperceptible smile and nod of what looked like gratitude. Before the bailiffs led him away, Wayne patted his shoulder reassuringly.

"Don't worry, man," Wayne said. "We're going to appeal this."

"No. Nobody's appealing anything" were Rayon's last words to them.

For the next eight years, he lived behind the walls of Great Meadow, Auburn, and Coxsackie maximum-security prisons. And beginning at Downstate Correctional Facility, where he was processed, Rayon learned to view his world through the narrow lenses of suspicion and retaliation. He honed his own wariness and bitterness into a sonic system to guide him through the maze of human deceit and savagery in which he was forced to maneuver every day. He avoided the enduringly amiable with the same obsession as he did the persistently malevolent. Relatively recent experience taught Rayon that people's attempts at congeniality was simply the prelude to deceitfulness. He came to accept that really nasty inmates and correction officers just wanted to meet their daily quota of people they could crap on. Sometimes in his reflective moments, Rayon seriously considered the possibility that he might be one of the nasty ones. But it didn't matter because his raging, violent demons had to be fed.

Rayon had always been tall and stocky. A standout football player in high school and in college, he had grown a little flabby during his eleven years as a Pentecostal minister. But eight years of working out in prison had transformed him into a spectacle of rippling muscles and arrogant brazenness. He barely remembered now his disciplined life of fervent prayer and devotion. His devotion shifted in prison to bodybuilding and strength development. Rayon looked at least fifteen years younger than his actual age of forty-one. He worked out alone with a ferociousness that discouraged even the most casual interaction. So he wasn't aware that an ominous new cloud of violence had settled into the facility.

Shorty Hernandez was a drug dealer from the Bronx who was doing a seven-to-twenty-year bid for illegal gun possession. He had a reputation for shooting his rivals in the face. The Bronx district attorney was never able to convict him on any of a half-dozen manslaughter and murder charges. However, they eventually convinced a former girlfriend to set him up. She disclosed some possible locations of his cache of weapons.

Shorty was a ruthless thug—even by prison standards. He was stocky, with close-cropped hair and was excessively tattooed. He probably had no idea how hilarious he looked trying to affect the exaggerated swagger his taller counterparts pulled off with so much more grace and ease. His significantly shorter legs just couldn't maintain the rhythm and glide his entourage of fellow Dominican Republic expatriates had perfected. Shorty just didn't have swag. He seemed to be always shuffling to their striding.

But what he lacked in height, he made up for in viciousness.

About a week after Shorty was transferred from the Downstate Processing Center in Fishkill, New York, to Coxsackie, he and his crew entered the gym during a basketball scrimmage. But instead of walking along the perimeter of the basketball court, he led his entourage onto the floor. They walked slowly and deliberately across the boards—a blatant act of provocation that went unchallenged. The echoes of the bouncing ball, the excited voices of competition, and the squeals of rubber against the floorboards gave way to a sudden, sullen silence. The ten sweaty men in green khakis looked like an eerie freeze-framed image on a giant television screen. Shorty walked directly toward Gill, a lanky dark-skinned young man in the middle of the court who was holding the basketball against his hip.

"What you looking at, asshole?" Shorty spat at him and sauntered over to stand directly under the young man's sweaty chin. "You got something on your mind, bro?"

"Nah. Nah, man," Gill answered, slowly shaking his head. "I ain't got nuttin' on my mind, man. I'm just trying to play some ball, man."

A few drops of Gill's sweat landed on Shorty's forehead as he shook his head.

"Yo, man!" Shorty screamed. "Why you shaking yo shit on me, bro?"

And before anyone could react, the five members of the entourage formed a tight circle around Shorty and the young ball player. One of them reached into his shirt, pulled out what looked like a spool of white gauze dressing, and quickly passed it to Shorty. Although the other players on the court couldn't see past the wall of green prison uniforms surrounding Gill, they knew how it would end. Experience taught them to step far away. Two members of the crew held Gill's arms behind him as Shorty repeatedly stabbed him in the chest and abdomen with the sharpened handle of a plastic spoon. The players heard Gill grunt several times before the sound of his body crumpling to the floor reached them. Shorty returned the bloody plastic sliver to an accomplice who stuck it into its gauze wad before slipping it back into his shirt. Then they leisurely sauntered out through the double doors on the far side of the gym.

They never saw Gill again after an area EMT unit eventually rushed him to the Albany Medical Center twenty miles away. Rumor and conjecture took over the second the emergency medical workers removed him from the gym. There was really no other way for the inmates to process issues or events taking place beyond their immediate environment. Speculation supremely governed the unknown and ultimately transformed itself into fact based on the most likely scenario.

In this case, the most widely accepted development was that the pair of correction officers responsible for the gym had locked themselves in the adjacent officers' weight room before the incident. And added to the intrigue was the fact that one CO was a white female partnered with an

African American male. The readily accepted version invariably dictated that they were too engrossed in making love to pick up on the commotion on the basketball court. Another prevalent theory had the tactical response and the emergency medical teams allowing Gill to bleed out once they learned the situation was simply another Latino-on-black assault. Or vice versa.

The attack was a calculated announcement that a new and significant player had arrived at the Coxsackie Maximum Security Correctional Facility. The inmate population immediately realized the basketball court stabbing wasn't happenstance. Shorty and his crew knew that the majority of basketball players did little else. They were young and energetic with a single purpose—doing the bulk of their time on the courts in the yard or in the gym. As a group, their ambitions did not go much beyond playing basketball, so it always trumped educational opportunities, unless acquiring a GED became a parole requirement. And the ballers were not usually gang connected because they paid little interest to prison politics. Although as a matter of survival, they remained peripherally aware of the inmate hierarchy.

The older inmates, however, were less energetic but more contemplative. These old heads were much too cynical to be impressed by new arrivals, despite their notorious street credentials. It had been ages since anyone considered the old dudes impressionable young bloods. These old heads were perpetual scholars. They analyzed prison, nationa, and international politics. They studied law, religion, correctional officers and one another. They cultivated and maintained interlocking circles of coalitions and interests. Although most of them never lost their edge. They remained poised to exploit any opening or perceived weakness. An old head once told Rayon that survival in prison was an ongoing chess game.

"You have to be constantly reading the board and thinking two or three moves ahead of the game."

But Shorty was also reading the board. His crew had already brought him up to speed on the identities and proclivities of the dominant Coxsackie players. And it became clear that he wanted Rayon's position. Rayon did not deal drugs or any material commodities at the facility. His product was influence.

"I'm like the power company, man," he would say. "What I sell is clean, reliable, and powerful. I'm like Central Hudson Gas and Electric, man. I hook you up to the right connection, and all you gotta do is flick the switch."

Although Rayon didn't have a posse, it was widely understood that a select few young inmates had found favor with Coxsackie's champion gladiator. As such, they wore this invisible veil of protection that gave them immunity from indiscriminate prison predators. This handful of protected inmates were either high school acquaintances or relatives of former church members. Gill was the baby brother of Clarence Gilmore, his drummer at Middletown's Solid Rock Everlasting Temple who had followed him to Bread of Life Fellowship Ministries in Newburgh. Before his incarceration, Gill had a relatively thriving crack cocaine distribution business in Middletown. But then he decided to establish some modest franchises in the rigidly regulated Newburgh drug market. His modest empire exploded within a month after several of his sales representatives were set up to sell crack to undercover agents. Everett Gilmore, the young transplanted Middletown entrepreneur never had a chance on the Newburgh streets. He was convicted of second-degree criminal possession and sentenced to three to ten years in state prison.

Gill's stabbing was a definite breach of protocol. That's because respect for established procedure ensured the maintenance of order and a certain level of predictability in the prison. Adherence to these laws were quite distinct from the institution's rules to which they were subjected. It was also accepted that there were consequences for violation of this clandestine rule of law. Rayon realized immediately that Shorty had sent him a blatant challenge. The prison teemed with anticipation for several days. But Rayon didn't have the convenience of a posse to conduct reconnaissance for him. So he was forced to rely on his own instincts to determine the best time and circumstances to retaliate. He would have to read the board very intently but discretely before making his move.

But Shorty made the first move.

Rayon operated one of two steam-pressing industrial machines in the prison's laundry for the past three years. It was a prestigious assignment. Both machines were against the wall of the large room and were separated by a bank of giant clothes dryers. Several of the twenty washing machines lining the walls whirled nosily. The incessant, deafening gyrating and rattling of the washers and dryers made normal conversation near impossible. A succession of inmates fed the silent machines or extracted laundry before cranking them up again. The laundry room remained animated, hectic, and deafening as inmates bellowed acknowledgments and instructions and roughhoused when they could, as they sorted laundry and wheeled overladen carts in and out. They moved through the great room as lines of ants toting picnic remnants back to the nest. Both pressers had unobstructed views of the room's entrance and of the activity within.

Rayon had always found this work assignment reassuring because it would be almost impossible for a resentful fellow inmate to sneak up on him. His back was literally always against the wall. And except for the intermittent billows of steam that rushed past his eyes as he operated the presser, he had eyes on the door.

Rayon was about to fish some bed linen from a laundry cart parked under his left arm when he noticed another overstuffed cart next to it. He instinctively shifted his gaze to his right to discover another cart piled high with dirty laundry. He immediately knew something was out of order. He only received freshly cleaned linen at his pressing station. Suddenly, a Latino inmate who had been lingering at a nearby folding table took two long strides, and quickly thumped against the side of the laundry cart nearest Rayon. Green prison wear immediately erupted from one cart then from the other, like the steamy geyser of surfacing whales.

A slender bald Latino inmate, with tattoos running up his neck and covering his skull, jumped out of the first cart, swinging a two-foot-long bathroom sink drainpipe. Rayon recognized him as one of Shorty's thugs. He flashed a mouthful of gold teeth as he sneered at Rayon while making a series of ineffective jabs at his face and midsection. As Rayon grabbed at the pipe, he realized he was trapped between the presser and the wall. He also realized that the tattooed, gold-toothed would-be assassin was only a distraction. That realization came with a sharp pinch in his neck followed by searing pain. He felt that bite and a similar penetrating pain in his back again and again.

The blood streaming down his neck and back into his clothes felt like sweat during a summer workout in the yard. He tried to swat away the attackers in front and behind him, but both arms felt unbearably heavy and then immobile. It was as if someone had chained his arms to his body. He was aware of the drainpipe connecting savagely with his face, but that bout of agony had not yet registered. The excruciating throbbing in his neck and back dominated his senses. Rayon fell to his knees, banging his head against the top of the hot steam presser. Then the lights faded to black.

Oh, God. I'm dying, aren't I?

What did you say?

I asked if I'm dying.

No. What did you say before that?

I said, "Oh, God."

Why?

What do you mean?

I mean, you never once called on God for the last eight years. As a matter of fact, you carried on as if God didn't exist for you.

Well, I didn't feel like he existed—especially not for me.

So why did you call him just then?

I don't know.

And why did you ask if you're going to die? Do you care if you live or die? It's not like you have anything to live for.

I'm not sure.

You don't seem to know much about anything, do you?

I guess not.

Rayon looked down at his crumpled, bloodied body sprawled on the laundry room floor. It was wedged between his pressing machine and the wall. Men in prison greens began forming a loose semicircle around his body. There was an atmosphere of heightened curiosity but observable detachment in the room. It felt deeply discouraging to Rayon. After all, everyone in the facility knew him. They could at least show a little more concern for him. But then, it wasn't as if he had any friends among the inmates milling around down there. However, Rayon could feel no rancor for the lack of compassion his fellow inmates were displaying down on the floor. He could not even conjure up the slightest animosity against his assassins. Instead, he became conscious of an overwhelming sensation of peace and of an abundant calming presence as he hovered above the commotions below.

So are you ready to die?

I thought I was. I just wanted to be with Emanuel. I couldn't wait to be with my son because I was dead to everything in this world and everything was dead to me. I was empty, dead inside.

Well, you made that abundantly clear.

Rayon saw one correctional officer then another run toward his body. He realized then that the stabbing had taken place only seconds earlier because of the time it took the officers to reach him. They had been standing in the hallway, just outside the laundry room entrance. It was actually a technical violation of their duties because they were supposed to be inside the room, supervising the inmates. But the laundry operation was so efficient that any supervision was perfunctory. Consequently, it was not unusual for correctional officers assigned to the laundry to spend their entire shift in the hallway, away from the constant din of the machines.

So you don't mind being dead if dying will connect you with Emanuel?

That's correct.

Well, unfortunately, your death will bring you no closer to being with him.

But why not? That's my only desire. I don't care about anyone or anything else.

I know that you now realize how flawed that attitude is, don't you? And where would this grand reunion take place? Certainly not in the presence of the Almighty. Have you descended into such spiritual decline that you somehow envisioned a scenario where you would be in the Redeemer's presence while still harboring such intense hatred, animosity and heartlessness?

You are right. I know that now.

Rayon watched dispassionately as the officers pushed through the crowd of inmates to get to his bleeding body behind the presser.

"Everyone on the line, now!" a female officer shouted. "C'mon, move it. Let's go!"

The men reluctantly, almost lethargically, shuffled out the door with robot-like precision. They mechanically formed two straight columns along the long unbroken yellow line that stretched down the gray cement hallway. Rayon saw his two attackers calmly falling into the lines. But he felt no animosity.

So I take it that you also know you wouldn't see Emanuel if you die on that floor?

Yes.

I thought you would. But even in this moment of enlightenment, do you know why you wouldn't see him if you die now?

No.

You wouldn't see Emanuel if you die because he is not dead.

He is not dead? But . . .

He's alive and well and being raised by the same deranged but loving and attentive woman who took him off the train eight years ago.

But how? Where are they? How is Emanuel?

They're living in Wheeling, West Virginia. The neighbors know the woman as an overprotective but doting single mother. Her name is Daishia and has blended very inconspicuously into her Nineteenth Street apartment building. People in Wheeling know her as a slightly eccentric, unwed mother. And Emanuel—she named him Jeremy—is a sweet, quiet, reflective eight-year-old boy.

Rayon hovered over the ambulance as it raced, screaming north up Route 9W toward Albany. He had now become extraordinarily invested in his own recovery because Emanuel was suddenly and miraculously alive. He felt overwhelmed as the long-buried paternal instincts of selfless love and protectiveness flooded his consciousness.

Rayon closely followed the surgical staff's every movement in the operating room. He minutely monitored every incision, every suture performed on his ravaged neck and upper torso. He had become so acutely apprehensive and distracted by the prospect of dying that he forgot he was not alone. He just knew that he couldn't die now—not now that he knew his son was alive. He had to live!

But the question is, what kind of life will you live if you survive this surgery? Can we expect a resurgence of your intolerable, immature, and hateful vehemence?

Will you acknowledge the irreversible damage and excruciating pain you have caused by your insufferable isolation from everyone who has ever loved you?

I know. I know. But I don't want to die without being with my son again.

It's not that easy. You can't just wish to be with Emanuel again, and presto, you have the desires of your heart. There is the matter of forgiveness. Remember the beautiful sermons you used to preach on forgiveness? But you never even considered forgiving Shantel for her selfishness. You never apologized to the Hills for killing their daughter. You never extended a smidgen of sympathy when your mother-in-law died. It never occurred to you to comfort your father when your mother suffered that debilitating stroke. We watched you becoming more entangled in your web of self-pity and hate. You allowed your obsession with hate for yourself and others to transform you into an unfeeling fighting machine that maimed weaker men. You openly disrespected God by your callous disregard for the suffering of others. Whatever happened to loving God with all your being and loving your neighbor as you love yourself?

I supposed I stopped loving myself so long ago that it became impossible to love anyone else—especially God.

Rayon became aware of a young intern's increasing frustration at the operating table. He complained hysterically to the surgical team that blood from a perforated lung had been seeping rapidly into the thoracic cavity and was seriously compromising the heart. The surgeon seemed agitated and indecisive because Rayon's vitals were deteriorating critically. He desperately needed the assistance of a more experienced emergency room surgeon. But it would be the second time that day a more seasoned colleague would have to bail him out. Another intervention so soon wouldn't look good on his evaluations.

Well, here you are at the crossroads. You have a choice. You can lose your life at the hands of this young man's indecisiveness and pride. Or you can be restored and resurrected into a whole new existence. What will it be?

I want to live.

Sure you do. But just uttering the words isn't enough. You know that God knows your heart, right? So before you say anything, make sure your words are coming from an honest and contrite heart. God can restore your body and leave you in better shape that you've ever been. But the question is, what will you do with this new and improved body? What kind of life will you live in this new body? How will you glorify God with your restored life?

I want to live so badly now. I will do whatever it takes.

Two surgeons immediately appeared at the operating table. One of them, a small man who radiated abundant nervous energy appeared to be upset and agitated. He barked something to his portly colleague, who reached up and readjusted the overhead surgical light. Although blue surgical masks obscured their faces, they projected a definite aura of authority as they examined Rayon's injuries. The agitated surgeon again barked a short indistinguishable comment to his colleague, who tapped the intern on his shoulder and motioned with his head for him to step away from the table. The young man walked out of the room hesitantly, a portrait of defeat and humiliation.

OK, here's what's happening. You actually clinically died a moment ago. But God prearranged your revival. That's why those two doctors are down there. They are instruments of God's grace and mercy.

Oh, thank you! Thank you!

You're wasting your thanks on me. I'm not the one who will restore your life.

Thank you, Father God! I thank you, and I praise you! I glorify you!

Hold up a minute. There's something you have to do before God allows those surgeons down there to suction that blood from your chest cavity. Can you see how it's collecting in there? But there's something you have to do before God allows them to restart your heart.

Just name it. I'll do it. I swear to God . . .

Oh my. Oh my. What does the Bible say about swearing to God? I know it has been a while for you, but I believe Matthew 5 and 34 says, "But I tell you, do not swear an oath at all: either by heaven, for it is God's throne." C'mon now, Bishop Hendricks, let's start off on the right foot.

I'm sorry. I'm so sorry.

All right. When you go back to prison, you can expect to serve out another eight years. There'll be no easy breaks for you. That's because you will need every minute of those eight years to prepare yourself for a ministry of evangelism and church planting when you walk out of the prison gates.

Eight years?

Yes, eight more years before you return to the outside. But during that time, you will minister to the men inside. You will spread the love of Jesus. You will radiate such love that even the hardest thugs will be attracted to your ministry. Even Shorty will become one of your staunchest disciples. But you have to prepare yourself spiritually and intellectually. You must become a scholar of the Apostle Paul. You must read and internalize everything he has written about evangelism and about planting churches. You must study in detail all of Paul's missionary journeys, paying particular attention not so much to his trials and tribulations but to the mind-set he maintained throughout his ministry. Are you prepared to be a true bishop to dozens then hundreds and then thousands when God opens the prison doors?

Yes, sir! But . . .

But what?

What about Emanuel?

Yes, Emanuel. God has arranged a miraculous reunion between the both of you just after his sixteenth birthday. God has determined that Emanuel needs the next eight years to work out some issues with his adopted mother before he can make room for you in his life.

Rayon and his angel watched in silence as the surgical team worked feverishly beneath them. It felt as if he were witnessing his own rebirth.

###

THE COERCIVE TRUSTEE

As soon as her cell phone alarm went off, Rosalie grabbed the wig off her night table and instinctively mashed it down on her head.

It was critical that no one saw her wigless—not even her husband—because the wigs hid a bald spot above her left temple. That permanent hairless patch reminded her of her helplessness and of her humiliation as a battered woman. She was a wife and childless person who, after fifteen years of marriage, passively absorbed violence in shameful silence. Rosalie was a tall slender light-skinned woman. At forty-one, she still looked convincingly like a fashion model. She loved beautiful clothes and worked out zealously to compliment her high-fashion wardrobe.

She took the phone into the farthest of the two guest bedrooms down the hallway from their room. She entered the bathroom, sat on the closed toilet, and called the Trenton Police Department and asked for Detective Dennis Briggs. A male dispatcher with a raspy, cheerless voice told her that Detective Briggs would not be available until Monday evening and asked if she would like to leave him a message. Rosalie thanked him, slipped the phone into her bathrobe pocket, and wandered noiselessly downstairs to the kitchen.

From the beginning, Anthony told Rosalie of his two major life goals: the expansion of his business into major Pennsylvanian cities and raising a son to continue his entrepreneurial legacy. But he wanted a son more than anything else. He talked about fathering a son as early as 1990, when they first met. And there was never any speculation about his forthcoming progeny. Back then, Anthony Junior was as real to him as his own social security number. Not only did he name him, but Anthony had already selected his son's nursery school and private elementary and high schools. But he remained conflicted about which Ivy League university he would entrust Anthony Junior's postsecondary education. It was always among

Princeton, Rutgers, and the University of Pennsylvania because he wanted to keep Anthony Junior close to home.

He made the bearing of a son Rosalie's commitment to him and to the marriage. In his vision, Anthony would continue to add to his chain of urban clothing stores and provide his family the most opulent lifestyle imaginable. All she had to do was continue to look fabulous and to provide him with at least one son. He desperately wanted the "and Son" he already added to the signs above his four stores to be real and meaningful.

And Rosalie had two major goals also. She intensely wanted a family, although she was not as particular as her husband. She had not established any predetermined number of children, nor did she have any gender-specific preferences. In addition, Rosalie wanted to complete her postgraduate studies and to earn a doctorate in education administration.

Rosalie blamed piña colada for her eventual marriage to Anthony. She claimed the drink took advantage of her unfamiliarity with alcohol and seduced her into acting more extroverted than normal. Her connection with Anthony came after she met some classmates at a bar on Walnut Street on an unusually warm May afternoon in 1990. They met to celebrate the completion of their education policy predoctorate program. Rosalie arrived late but found a place at the periphery of the small but boisterous group. She listened as her colleagues recounted their graduate school horror tales. Although it was barely midafternoon, the absence of natural light in the bar discouraged any feelings of celebration in her.

The dismal atmosphere only heightened Rosalie's anxiety about her uncertain academic future. She was twenty-six, a perpetual student with two years ahead of her before completing a doctoral program, and preoccupied with grants and loan applications. Every spare moment was consumed with incessant searches for paid fellowships. But the competition was ferocious. So Rosalie remained too preoccupied with her bleak economic future to feel very festive that afternoon. However, no one else in the room seemed to share her melancholy. The stories reinforced her classmates' collective victory over impossible assignments, rigid professors, abject poverty, and the delicate balancing act that made their survival possible.

Rosalie tried desperately to find the same level of hilarity as her colleagues as she sipped on her glass of tonic water and lime. Sure, she felt the same feelings of relief and accomplishment as they did, but all she could conjure up was a faint intermittent smile when anyone looked in her direction.

Then someone wrestled the tonic water from her hand and replaced it with a tall glass of piña colada. It was love at first sip. There was no instant assault of scorching, gagging alcohol as in her previous attempts at adult drinking. The smooth, creamy texture reminded her of the coconut-flavored ice cream she loved as a child. A little later, as she chewed on the pineapple slice she fished from the empty glass, Rosalie wondered how she would get another drink.

Halfway through her second drink, Rosalie thought she had a brilliant idea for pranking one of their professors. She pushed her way to the center of the group and held up her glass for recognition. She felt uncommonly light, congenial, and even funny.

"Em, what do you all think of giving Professor Atkinson a fashion makeover?" Rosalie asked.

There was an immediate eruption of boisterous laughter. Prof. Archibald Atkinson was a caricature of the stereotypical college professor. He was tall, lanky and amusingly disheveled. He wore the same brown bowtie for as far back as anyone could remember. But his hallmark fashion statement was the dark-gray-and-brown tweed jacket and the same pair of brown corduroy pants he lived in year round.

"I would absolutely kill to see Professor Atkinson in a bright-yellow jacket with some green slacks!" Rosalie shouted at the crowd.

The raucousness was deafening. And she was experiencing a moment of anxiety-free lightheadedness. Soon, the events following her suggestion in the bar that evening were blurry. But it was early evening rush hour when she and five other students entered the brightly lit store on Market and North Fifty-Seventh streets. Rosalie couldn't believe these marginally sane and reasonably intelligent people were taking her dizzy suggestion so literally. But what the heck; it sounded like fun. Some guy in the bar had given them the address of the hottest, ghetto-fabulous clothing store in Philadelphia. So here she was, with five white people, clothes shopping for a geeky white man, who would definitely not be amused.

But they never bought Professor Atkinson the yellow-and-green ensemble. Because a wave of nausea clouted Rosalie as soon as she entered the uncomfortably humid store. She immediately leaned against a revolving rack of colorful shirts to steady herself. But the clothes rack rotated under the abrupt addition of her weight, shifting Rosalie off-balance and tumbling her to the floor. As she fell, she tasted the coconut flavor, scorching rum, and acrid stomach acids rising up from her throat and filling her mouth. She instinctively slapped an opened hand to her mouth, but the rancid white liquid was already seeping through her fingers, down her neck and into her clothes.

Rosalie squeezed her eyes tightly shut as if to expel some embedded pain. But the pain she actually felt was the ache of humiliation. She remained immobile on the floor, eyes closed, her body folded into a fetal position. She heard the sounds of concern, confusion, and some revulsion above her. The vomit had saturated the top of her denim shirt. Then she became aware of the sounds of approaching rapid footsteps transmitted through the thick industrial carpet then the sound of a rich, comforting baritone voice just above her.

"Are you hurt, miss?"

Rosalie didn't respond but squeezed her eyes tighter and attempted to tuck her knees closer into her chest.

"Did you hit your head? Do you think you hurt anything when you fell?"

Rosalie raised her head off the floor far enough to shake her head. "No."

The voice had drawn much closer. She smelled his cologne and noted a subtle aroma suggesting a delicate earthiness that evoked tropical fruit groves.

"OK. That's good," the voice purred. "Just stay where you are, and I'll get someone to clean you up. OK?"

She heard his retreating footsteps and the same voice barking orders for someone to clean up the customer.

A young female sales associate immediately appeared to escort Rosalie to a restroom. She didn't open her eyes until the young woman stepped out of the room and closed the door. When Rosalie apprehensively left the restroom, she was wearing a donated but oversized beige man's shirt to replace her soiled shirt.

She stepped out of the restroom to see the face that was connected to the voice. The face smiled at her, exposing bright white teeth and a pair of full lips surrounded by a carefully manicured moustache and neatly trimmed beard. His close-cropped, expertly edged haircut betrayed the contour of a man who was fastidious about his appearance. Rosalie also thought she had detected a face that projected gentleness and compassion during that brief scrutiny. She struck him as a man used to exercising authority while maintaining his humility and a high degree of benevolence.

Despite her protests, he insisted on personally taking her to Mercy Philadelphia Hospital's emergency room on South Fifty-Fourth Street. By the time he took her to her apartment, Rosalie was convinced she had met the most compassionate and attractive man on the planet.

What Rosalie saw was a carefully sculptured image that took Anthony several months to hone. He desperately wanted to shed the street-hustler, player-pimp image he successfully sold every day to impressionable young black men. That look played very well in the clubs. But Anthony wanted a more sophisticated image. He realized he had matured tremendously over the three years since he took ownership of the store. He had no problem selling ridiculous peacock-colored clothes to shallow dudes off the block. But that didn't mean he had to look and act like them. He had resolved to put those days behind him. Anthony was determined to look and to act differently. And although he couldn't articulate it, he knew what he wanted. He wanted to evoke the appearance of an urbane, cultured entrepreneur. So he tooled and retooled his appearance by studying magazine photographs of famous black men he admired. And in the end, it was Billy Dee Williams, the actor, who became his architype.

But Anthony's hustle was always about clothes. That's how he got his start—by boosting merchandise in small busy stores. The *Super Fly* era was still flourishing when he showed up in Philadelphia in 1983. He was nineteen years old. Most of the men he saw in the clubs were trying to look like players or pimps. They had to affect the mack daddy look to be taken seriously. Everyone who wanted to be somebody had to have a macked-out Cadillac with customized chrome grille, ornate interiors, and outrageous hood ornaments, like cow horns and boomerang TV antennas on the trunk.

But it was the pimp fashion that fascinated Anthony. It was riveting to him that a guy could step out of a glitzy Caddy in the middle of the week, wearing a canary-yellow three-piece suit with matching yellow hat and yellow alligator shoes. Some of these players had fur-lined capes to match every flamboyantly colored suit in their closets. He realized that in this world of ostentatious fashion extravagance, there were no defined male-color restrictions. Players could wear blushing-pink, blood-red, lime-green, or canary-yellow suits with no fear of being considered effeminate. It was all about perfecting the confident swagger to pull it off. Anthony recognized he was on the periphery of a bright, dazzling world where the intensity of color ruled. He also realized that there was an infinitesimally small number of fashion originals presiding over a multitude of imitators.

And there was money to be made if he could somehow meet the fashion needs of the masses of impressionable young inner-city men. Anthony took note of the cheap imitators gawking on the sidewalks as the bona fide players entered the clubs with their parasitic entourages. He saw the copycats inside the clubs sucking on bottles of cheap Ballantine or Coors beer while staring longingly at the pimps and players sipping Hennessy and Dom Perignon.

His life's destiny had become finding a way to create the illusion of street royalty for the susceptible masses of young Philadelphians. Anthony originally didn't have even the glimmer of a plan, only a burning desire to supply the demand for colorful urban fashion. But he had to start somewhere.

His business plan was extraordinarily uncomplicated. He would accumulate a substantial stash of money and somehow find a supplier of affordable ghetto-fabulous clothing. Anthony launched the first part of his strategy with the same degree of fundamental artlessness as his business plan. Initially, he would saunter into clothing stores along Broad or Market streets, grab shirts or slacks off the racks, and hide them inside his coat before casually stepping out to the sidewalk. He would then walk over to Rittenhouse Square and try to sell the stolen merchandise to white college students for a fraction of the cost. But the pickings had become disastrously slim after a while because he was running out of small stores to rip off. That's because store workers began to recognize Anthony and would chase him off the premises.

One spring morning, Anthony was walking along Market Street, trolling for vulnerable clothing stores. He crossed to the other side of the street near North Fifty-Seventh Street when he spotted a small store that had previously escaped his attention. A faded sign that stretched across the entire front said Malinowitz & Son Gentlemen's Haberdashers Since 1943. He glanced inside as he walked slowly past the entrance. It was dark and cluttered with no visible attendants—all favorable conditions for a desperate thief.

Anthony walked to the corner of Fifty-Seventh Street, abruptly turned around and headed back toward the store. Four naked low-wattage light bulbs suspended on dusty cords and the opened doorway provided the only light inside. There were three long rows of cluttered clothes racks, crammed with dark-colored clothing. The center row, filled with black and gray suits, hung sadly and silently, as if waiting to be fitted on dead men. Tuxedos in assorted styles filled the right and left rows. The center row presented more variety and the only hint of brightness on display. It featured formal, white shirts with plain and frilly fronts. A rack of pants at the rear of the store attempted to flaunt some variety. There were black stripes on gray and gray stripes on black. The store was dark, gloomy, and depressing, as if it catered exclusively to sad, old, white men with hypomanic disorders.

Anthony zipped through the store quickly and was about to exit to the sidewalk when he heard a voice from somewhere in the darkness.

"Hey you, Mr. Speedy Gonzales," a raspy voice called out. "Wait a minute."

Anthony stopped abruptly and looked hastily around the gloomy store.

"Who that?" he responded, his voice betraying a trace of anxiety. "Where you at, man? Don't play with me!"

"What's the matter?" the voice said. "You want I should come down to you? Come over here."

Anthony turned his head in the direction of the gravelly voice. It came from a raised, enclosed platform in a front corner of the store. He peered into the darkness to see a white-bearded, round-faced man wearing a black yarmulke.

"Yo, man," Anthony called across the room at him. "You trying to scare somebody?"

"Why should I scare you? You think maybe I should be scaring you?"

"I don't know, man. What you want, shadow man?"

"Shadow man, he calls me," the man said somberly. "Well, shadow man I am then. But please, come over here."

Anthony slowly and deliberately made his way to the enclosed platform. It was about two feet above the floor with a narrow counter on which sat an antique manual National cash register surrounded by a clutter of paperwork. Although the man wearing the yarmulke was standing, Anthony could barely see him. The man was short and round, his white shirt straining against his gut. He stood out in glaring contrast to the shadowy darkness around him. He had been perfectly hidden in the dark and behind the stacks of paperwork on the counter. Anthony now stood at the base of the platform, looking up at the mysterious yarmulke man.

"So what's up, man?" Anthony said. "What you want?"

"What I want?" he replied. "I'll tell you what I want. What I want is for you to tell me why you didn't steal from me."

"Say what?" Anthony screamed.

"I want to know why you didn't try to steal from me."

"Wow! You're one crazy old man. Why would you ask me that?"

"Well, you're a thief . . ."

"Hold up. Hold up, old man. You don't even know me. Why you up there calling me a thief, man?"

"You ask me why? I'll tell you why. For forty-five years, I sit right here. I watch people come, and I watch people go. Do they see me? Only those who know I'm here. In that time, I get to know who comes to buy and who comes to steal."

"So what you saying? You know I come in here to steal?"

"Again you ask, so I answer. Yes, I know you come to steal."

"Why you say that?"

"Here you go. Always with the questions. Why I say that? I say that because you look like a thief. You walk like a thief. Therefore, you are a thief. Forty-five years taught me to know a thief from a customer."

"OK, old dude. If you know I'm a thief, what you want from me?

"You call me old dude, I call you young thief. OK, young thief, I'll tell you what I want from you. I want to know why you didn't try to steal my merchandise."

"You kidding, right, man?"

"Kidding? Who's kidding? What, I look like Steve Allen or George Burns to you? Look, a thief walks into my store and walks out without even touching anything. Is it so crazy I want to know why?"

"OK. OK. I dig where you're coming from, old dude. Let's say I was a thief. Why in the world would I want to steal any of your crap, man?"

"Crap? You say my clothes are crap?"

"Yeah, dude. It's all crap."

"Mr. Clothes Thief, you stand in my store and tell me everything in here is crap?"

"You ask me, right? And I'm just telling you."

"Mr. Clothes Expert, did you see the names of the people who make my suits? I have Loro Piana, I have Turnbull and Asser, I have Bill Blass, and I have Hugo Boss. I even have Pierre Cardin. Did you ever hear of these people? Did you feel the quality of the material, Mr. Expert?"

"Didn't have to dude. It's all funeral clothes, man."

"Let me tell you something, Mr. Thief Man." His voice was grave and raspy, betraying his agitation. "Me and my father before me, we sell the finest men's clothes in Philadelphia. The best material. Clothes fit for ambassadors and aristocrats. Such a list of satisfied customers, you won't believe."

"Oh yeah?" Anthony asked incredulously. "So where are they, old dude? Ain't nobody in here but me and you."

There was a long pause. Anthony heard the *thonk, thonk* of a clock's pendulum in the semidarkness, somewhere within the enclosed platform.

The yarmulke man then turned toward the back of the darkened interior of the enclosed platform.

"This I have to also hear from this *cachem attick*?" he said. "Is it not enough that I hear it from you every day?"

"Hey, man," Anthony called up to him. "What you call me?"

"He called you a wise guy," a woman's voice responded from the darkness. "You're right, I'm right and he's wrong. He's old, stubborn and wrong."

"Hold it. Hold it, y'all." Anthony said. "I ain't getting in the middle of no family thing. But I'm just telling you, man, this is a dead store for dead people. Ain't nothing in here for the living."

"Ah, what does a thief from the street know?" the yarmulke man said. "Does he have a business? Does he know my business? Did he graduate from business school? I'll tell you what school he graduated from. He graduated from thief school."

"Hey, old dude," Anthony said. "I don't need this hassle. You the one who called me back inside this dead-ass store."

"Hirsh," the woman's voice called out from the darkness. "You know the boy is right. No, he didn't go to business school. No, he don't know your business. But you know what, Hirsh Malinowitz? It don't take a business school graduate to know this place died years ago."

"You, stop talking that death talk about my father's store," he said angrily, turning in the direction of the voice behind him. "I promised my father I would always keep his name in front of this store. You want I should break my word to him now? You, go back to your work. You, thief boy, go steal somewhere else."

"*A broch!* What promise?" the woman's voice shrieked from behind Malinowitz. "What name?"

"Listen, y'all," Anthony said breezily. "It's been real, but this ain't none of my business. Y'all keep it all in the family. See ya."

"No. No," the woman called out. "Stay right there, boy..."

"Boy!" Anthony shouted back. "Who you calling boy?"

"Sorry, mister, sir," she responded soothingly but never emerging from the darkness. "But you can't leave now. I believe the Lord sent you here to tell this stubborn old *alter kocker* what our sons, me, everybody's been telling him. Sell the business, Hirsh. Take what you can get for it and retire. It's not like he needs this. The man owns every building on the block."

"I'll tell you one thing," Malinowitz said, the defeat and resignation evident in his voice. "I'm glad my father isn't alive to hear you call his son an *alter kocker*. So what? I'm an old fart for wanting to hold on to my father's legacy?"

"Thank God your father had enough sense to rent out the other buildings on the block," she said. "We have a good life with the rents. Why you need this aggravation, Hirsh?"

"Aye. Aye. Aye," Malinowitz wailed, clasping his face between his plump hands. "Does it ever end with you? The complaining. The griping. The nagging. You will never understand, Chaya, what it is for a son to promise a father."

"What promise, Hirsh?" Chaya wailed from behind her husband. "It's a dead promise to a dead man about a dead store. Who cares anymore?"

"You have no heart, no kindness, Chaya," Malinowitz groused. "What little heart you had got drained out of you, little by little, when Jonathan moved to New York and then Mikhail went to Baltimore."

It sounded to Anthony like the latest episode of a protracted debate between Chaya and Hirsh Malinowitz. It was getting late and he hadn't made enough money to buy his first meal of the day. These old Jews could fight over the future of this sad store, but he had a whole day of hustling ahead of him. He turned and was halfway to the door when Chaya called to him.

"Mr. Young Man, sir," she called out. "One minute, please."

Anthony turned around to see a short skeletal woman emerge from the darkness.

"Our own sons don't want the store," she said. "They moved away with their families."

Chaya Malinowitz invited Anthony to join them in the dark wall-less office on the platform. And by the time he stepped back into the sunlight two hours later, he had reluctantly agreed to work for the Malinowitzs. But Anthony's reluctance to walk up those three steps to the platform office was far from genuine. He instinctively knew what she wanted and how the meeting would play out the instant Chaya requested he join them. He sensed she had emotionally abandoned the store decades ago and resented having to stare down into its apparent paralysis day after dreary day. This was a woman who sat in obvious frustration for years, waiting for a miracle that would free them from the shackles of Hirsh's commitment. Anthony realized he was Chaya's miracle.

The discussions were initially taxing and sluggish. It was mostly a vigorous debate between Chaya and Hirsh about maintaining the integrity of his father's legacy. Chaya spoke enthusiastically about her newfound vision for the store. She saw the store's aisles jammed with black people happily selecting armfuls of clothing from the racks. After all, only a handful of white people still lived in the neighborhood. She envisioned bright lights throughout the store reflecting colorful clothes and a bevy of cashiers relentlessly ringing up sales. Hirsh, however, saw the store quickly becoming unrecognizable with this proposed onslaught of alien customers hunting through the racks for outlandish merchandise. He lamented that he could feel his father's intense disapproval for even having the conversation.

"Meshugginer!" Hirsh wailed at one point. "Chaya, this is crazy talk. You want I should turn my father's store over to this *fremder*? He's a stranger, and the only thing we know about him is that he's a thief."

Anthony sensed that his best strategy was to stay out of the discussion unless asked specific questions.

"Hirsh. Hirsh," Chaya responded. She stood up and made a sweeping gesture with a wrinkled, boney arm. "Your father's store? You could do worse than bring in a stranger. Look at your father's store, Hirsh. When was the last time somebody bought something from your father's store? Or came in, even?"

Anthony wasn't sure at which point Hirsh ceded the store's fate to his wife, but within minutes, Chaya was thumbing through a packed worn Rolodex looking for painters, electricians, and other tradespeople. Hirsh reluctantly gave her the names of a few contemporary clothing wholesalers.

"Such people I would not speak to," Hirsh said with an air of resignation. "With their warehouses full of red trousers and green shoes. That's clothes? Who wears such clothes?"

But within two weeks, Malinowitz & Son Gentlemen's Haberdashers Since 1943 had become unrecognizable. Chaya emerged from the darkness of the elevated office to supervise the removal of the store's entire inventory. She sold it, at way below cost, to family and business friends.

Chaya seemed to be reborn, reenergized and inspired once she stepped into the light. She oversaw the installation of a brightly lit, new glass-encased show window that replaced the gloomy office. Everything dark or shadowy was transformed into bursts of brilliant yellow, florescent green, or glaring white. The warm colors created an illusion of expansion. And even before the new paint had dried, she was directing the placement of two dozen plastic-covered racks of brightly colored suits, jackets and slacks she had ordered earlier with Anthony's help.

Hirsh never entered the store after the meeting with his wife and Anthony. He made only one demand: that the name Malinowitz & Son Gentlemen's Haberdashers Since 1943 would never be removed. Anthony, who initially lived in a renovated storeroom at the back of the store, managed the operation under a commission arrangement with the Malinowitzs.

The store became an instant hit with the city's authentic players and its wannabe hustlers. Anthony convinced Chaya to stock the most bizarre outfits in the most outlandish colors they could find. He wanted to establish the Malinowitz & Son brand as the place that catered to Philadelphia's most eccentric, ghetto-fabulous demographic. And Anthony projected the brand. From the beginning, there was never the contradiction of the clothes salesman looking tacky. Those days were behind him. The dichotomy of the shoe salesman wearing busted sneakers would never again be his reality. He picked six new suits off the racks every week to strut along the now-red-carpeted floor. At first, Anthony stood outside the store in new colorful outfits, unconsciously tugging his shirt cuffs under his jacket sleeve. He kept up a perpetual stream of inviting dialogue with every black passersby—very much the carnival barker.

"Yo, brother man," he would say. "And how are you doing this fine morning? Lookie here, brother, I see you eyeing my threads. Hey! Hey!

Don't walk away today and be sorry tomorrow, my man. Check it out. Check it out, my brother. I can hook you up with a suit, matching brim and some boss kicks. Brother, you'll be so clean after I hook you up, people will think you showered in Clorox. And best of all, you'll still have money in your pocket."

But Anthony didn't have to do his sidewalk barking for long. Soon, the store remained so packed, especially on Saturdays, that he convinced Chaya to hire helpers. Anthony managed the store for two profitable years. Within three months, he moved from the renovated storeroom to an apartment in Center City. Nine months later, he bought a previously-owned beige-and-black Lincoln Continental with whitewall tires. It remained conspicuously parked in front of the store and was mysteriously never towed despite mountains of parking violations.

Anthony was having a good life. The store was a gold mine, and under a commission arrangement he had worked out with Chaya, he believed he was making as much money as any midlevel pimp. He owned a sweet-looking ride, had access to all the clothes he wanted, and had more women than he had ever imagined possible.

Then, one morning, he heard Chaya cough. It didn't bother him at first. She was an old woman, and old women coughed sometimes. But she coughed again and then had a more prolonged bout of raspy, incessant eruptions. Anthony became immediately concerned because not once in their two-year relationship had Chaya stayed home because of illness. She would be already in the glass-walled office when Anthony walked in every morning. And she left when he did at night to drop off the receipts in the bank's night deposit box. But he had never associated the old woman with any form of fragility before. True, she was gaunt to the bone, but she seemed to have the endurance of a racehorse and the agility of a mountain goat. Unlike the days when she sat in the shadows behind Hirsh, she was now everywhere, fixing, straightening, and helping. It seemed that the renovated store miraculously rejuvenated her.

Chaya's intermittent coughing bouts immediately immobilized Anthony. He quickly walked out of the store to sit behind the wheel of his parked car.

Whoa! Whoa! Time out. If Chaya gets sick and maybe dies, that'll be all she wrote. The old man and the lame sons will come down here in a jack flash and snatch away my good thing. Ain't nothing I can do about it because ain't nothing here with my name on it. Nah, man, nah. I ain't going down like that. Yo, man, you been settling for crumbs all your life, bro. It's time for you to enjoy piece of the pie.

Anthony returned to the store and immediately walked into the office and sat in the only other chair. Chaya looked across the cluttered desk at him and intuitively knew this was not going to be a routine progress report.

"Anthony, everything OK? You look *ajateytad*. You look troubled. Why you look so anxious?"

"Look, Chaya, I was just thinking. I been with you in the store for a minute, right?"

"A minute you say? I say many, many minutes," Chaya said frowning, a look of bewilderment covering her gaunt face.

"Well, you know what I mean. And in the time I've been here, was I good to you, to the store? Was I good for the business?"

"Anthony. Anthony," she answered, coming from behind the desk to stand in front of him. "Such a question. Why would you ask such a question?"

"Well, I'm just asking."

"It's better you should ask, Would I like to taste a bacon and cheese sandwich someday—just once? Or would I like to be twenty-two again for a day, than you should ask if you are good for the business."

Chaya touched Anthony's head and gently turned it with two fingers toward the glass plate overlooking the floor.

"Look down there. Tell me what you see," she said. But before he could answer, she said, "I see people. I see racks and racks of clothes. I see people taking those clothes from the racks and paying for them."

"Yeah," Anthony said, twisting his body in the chair to face the store. "Yeah, you're right. People out there buying clothes."

"So tell me, *boychick*, why the crazy question about you and the business?"

"Well," Anthony said, still looking out on the shop floor. "I'm just thinking about me. You know, it's real good now. I ain't complaining. But if something happens to you, I'm out on my ass."

"If something happens to me? What is this *something* you think will happen to me? You think maybe I catch something and die tonight, boychick?"

A week later, when Anthony walked into the office, Chaya was already there, as usual; but she was not filing receipts into one of the metal cabinets or reviewing inventory sheets. Anthony found her sitting primly and uncharacteristically calm behind her desk. A pink Jackie Kennedy-like pillbox hat sat squarely on her head as if waiting for the rightful owner to claim it. Strands of stringy gray hair drooped unevenly from under the hat. Her clasped white-gloved fingers rested uncomfortably and prayerlike on the desk in front of her. A pink satin dress with a high collar that reached her earlobes threatened to swallow her tiny frame. She looked comically regal and fragile.

"What going on, Chaya?" Anthony asked, not attempting to mask his confusion. "Why you all dressed up? Something wrong? Hirsh OK?"

"Oy vey," Chaya said, looking at Anthony with mock horror. "All these questions, boychick."

"Well, I mean, you're all dressed up. You never dress up to come to the store. I just want to know what's up. That's all."

"So an old lady can't put on her Shabbat best on a Monday? Is there some law that says an old lady can't put on a nice dress every now and then? You dress up every day."

Chaya let him stew in confusion and bewilderment for several minutes while she sat behind her desk, looking at Anthony and wearing a saintly smile.

She stood up after a while, stuck an oversized clutch bag under her arm, and stepped away from the desk.

"Come on, boychick, let's go for a ride," she said.

Chaya told Anthony to drive to Logan Square and didn't speak again until he asked if she wanted a specific building. She directed him to an impressive office building on Cherry and Eighteenth streets and instructed him to let her out and to find a parking garage. She fished a law office business card out of a purse in her bag and told him to meet her in the waiting room. Fifteen minutes later, they were sitting next to each other in the chic waiting room of Deacon, Kassner and Malinowitz.

They were a curious couple, siting among the half dozen people scattered within the gray marble and glass-walled room. A diminutive, elderly, Jewish woman was nervously bouncing a faux-leather clutch bag on her lap. On the adjoining chair was an imposing black man with a beige fedora firmly planted on his head. The jacket of his double-breasted brown silk suit, firmly buttoned but revealing a pink-and-white striped shirt under a wide emerald silk tie. As Anthony sunk into the chrome-and-leather waiting room chair, he smoothly rested one leg over his knee. The movement intentionally exposed blood-red silk socks emerging from brown, python slip-ons.

Chaya and Anthony were eventually ushered into an expansive office with dark mahogany wall panels, towering bookshelves built into the walls and the longest pair of burgundy leather sofas Anthony had ever seen. And across the room, a paunchy, balding, bespectacled man arose from behind a massive mahogany desk and strode across the thickly carpeted floor with outstretched arms toward them.

"Aunt Chaya," he said, hugging and gently rocking her. "I told you, you didn't have to come here. I would come to your house."

"Come to my house, he says," Chaya said, turning to Anthony. "I should ask the busiest lawyer in Philadelphia to drop everything and come to my house."

"Why not?" he asked Anthony. "For her, I would go across the country on a bicycle if she would ask. You are my uncle's wife. You and Uncle Hirsh, after all you did for me? College. Law school. I can't do enough. Really."

"Michael, enough already," she chided him. "It was nothing. You needed help. We're family. That's all."

Michael released her and patted a place on one of the sofas for her. Anthony sat on the sofa across from them.

"This is Anthony, the young man I told you about," she said, beckoning Anthony to join them on the giant sofa. She patted him on the shoulder when he took his seat next to her. "He's a business genius, this Anthony. And he never spent a minute in business school."

Anthony smiled and reached forward to grasp Michael's outstretched pudgy hand. It was firmer than he expected.

"Well, all I can say is, if my Aunt Chaya is a fan, then you're OK with me," Michael said as he eased back into the crackling leather. "If you hadn't come along, my Uncle Hirsh would still be schlepping down to that depressing cave he called a store."

Anthony just smiled and nodded sheepishly. He found everything about the building, the people, and the office peculiar and intimidating. This was not his element. He knew nothing about this world or how he was expected to navigate his way through this maze of rich white people. Hell, he didn't even know why he was up here in this snazzy law office. He was instinctively suspicious of Chaya's lawyer nephew and with all his compliments. He refused to be embraced by the sofa's seductive opulence. Instead, Anthony maintained his perch on the edge of the overstuffed cushion. He was trying to anticipate just what kind of setup he was in for.

But as it turned out, Chaya had asked her nephew to draft an agreement that would allow Anthony to eventually own the store. Her sons were, at best, ambivalent about the store's future, largely because it had an adverse impact on their past. It was undoubtedly a major source of the family's income and ensured rewarding college educations and trips to Israel and Europe. But the shop also represented childhood servitude and estrangement from their parents during most of their formative years. It would be a blessing if someone would be willing to take it.

"Hell, I'd give the damned thing away if it would mean my mother could spend more time with her grandchildren," Jonathan said during a telephone call that weekend with his parents about the disposition of the store.

Michael Malinowitz explained to Anthony that Hirsh and Chaya were willing to lease the store to him with an option to buy the property for $550,000 over five years. According to the agreement he retrieved from his desk, Michael emphasized the $150,000 annual payments, which he suggested, could be divided into monthly disbursements of $12,500 to include interest and taxes.

"All my uncle asks is that you retain the store's original name at least until you own it outright," Michael said.

Anthony was in shock. He remembered signing several documents afterward. And he was aware of a trace of embarrassment about the effort it took to produce his signature and how primitive it appeared. But as they rode back to the store, his bewilderment shifted to euphoria as Chaya explained the magnitude of the law office meeting. He was a property owner now. He was a businessman. He was somebody! He was no longer the tail; he was the head. He was no longer the help; he was the boss!

Anthony felt invincible as he swerved through the city's midday traffic. He barely heard Chaya as she prattled excitedly about how blessed she was when he walked into the store two years ago. She related for the umpteenth time how he freed her from the monotony and the gloom of the store. He was a brash, hungry and desperate twenty-one-year-old clothes thief when he walked into Hirsh and Chaya's lives. And now at twenty-three, he was on the verge of owning his own piece of the pie. He smiled as he slowed the car down for a red light and tuned in to Chaya again.

"Don't get me wrong," she said, the excitement in her voice unmistakable. "I love my husband. Love him for fifty years. But *oy vey iz mir*. Every day, every day, the same thing. I sit in the dark behind Hirsh. When business was good, it wasn't so bad. Boring, but not so bad. But the neighborhood, it changed. Regular customers, not so regular anymore. And Hirsh. Poor Hirsh. He just sits there, day after day, hoping, praying, and mourning for his old customers."

Anthony kept nodding his head, pretending to be listening intently. But his mind could not comprehend or accommodate her dark, boring history.

"And you know how I spent my days? No, my years?" Chaya continued. "I spent my time praying in the dark for freedom. I prayed for a miracle."

She leaned over and punched Anthony lightly on his arm.

"And you, *ziskeit*," she whispered. "You are my miracle."

"Zis what?"

"Sweetheart," she replied.

Three years later, Anthony was twenty-six and already thinking of expanding his business to other predominantly black neighborhoods. He had already taken Michael Malinowitz's family rates offer to enlist the law firm whenever necessary. The firm was representing Anthony in a lease arrangement of a larger retail space on East Chelten and Germantown avenues in Germantown. So when he met Rosalie, Anthony, as far as he knew, was the youngest clothing store owner in Philadelphia.

She was twenty-seven, a year older than Anthony, but was blown away by his maturity and charisma and, as she admitted later, was seductively intimidated by his business intellect. She spent much of that summer at the store, observing him and being in awe of his organization and management skills. She loved to study his interaction with customers and employees, especially how he blended his decisiveness with gentleness. She thought he would make a great father. Rosalie cherished his patience and indulgence with her since she was convinced she must have been the most sexually inexperienced and inhibited woman he had ever been with.

Anthony loved Rosalie's analytical mind. It fascinated him that she could take the most innocuous observations and present them to him with startling new insights. He greedily absorbed her views on politics, religion, and especially education. Conversations with Rosalie were nothing like the barbershop banter to which he was exposed for all his life. Although she was effortlessly articulate and carefully instructive, Anthony never felt she was condescending. He found himself recycling her thoughts and opinions to business associates and golfing acquaintances. Because he had always been a quick study, Rosalie's intellectual influence allowed Anthony newfound respect as a bright young businessman. And he liked that she showed genuine interest in his growing business and in his personal growth and social development.

They married during Rosalie's Christmas break later that year. It was a small ceremony at a banquet hall in Ardmore, outside Philadelphia. She had only a small handful of college friends and her parents, who flew in from Illinois. And Anthony invited the Malinowitzs and a few store employees. Rosalie had mentioned a Caribbean honeymoon, but Anthony said it would require him getting a passport. And he was not prepared to do that. They spent a week, instead, in Key West, Florida.

She did achieve one of her goals—a PhD from Princeton University. But it was becoming increasingly evident that, barring some miracle, after fifteen years, motherhood would be elusive—if at all. Three years into the marriage, they had already made the rounds of fertility specialists in Pennsylvania, Connecticut, New York, and New Jersey. And it was after one of those trips that Rosalie caught the first glimpse of Anthony's volatile nature.

They were returning to Philadelphia from another disappointing consultation in New York City. They had been riding in silence on the New Jersey Turnpike for almost an hour. It was midafternoon but the six-lane highway seemed unusually isolated. Before the cloud of silence had enveloped the car, Rosalie had been trying to rise above the heavy smoldering depression with which she had been wrestling since they left the city. She was desperately looking for some glimmer of sunshine in this dark situation. She had told Anthony before that she was willing to explore other options. But her husband was resolute about his heir being his "own flesh and blood." Although she attempted to have the adoption conversation previously, Rosalie was never able to get it off the ground. Meanwhile, Anthony had not spoken since they left the specialist's office on Manhattan's Upper West Side. The car's elaborate, custom-built stereo system remained unusually mute. Rosalie eventually spoke at the windshield, not looking at her husband.

"You know, Anthony," she said. "I was just thinking. This doesn't have to be as bad as it seems."

Anthony didn't respond but he looked intently at the empty stretch of highway ahead of him.

"Are you listening, Anthony?"

He still didn't acknowledge her, but his response was to gun the engine, swerve into the extreme left passing lane for no apparent reason and then pull back into his original lane.

"What was that about?" she asked, the apprehension apparent in her voice.

"You want to know what that's about?" Anthony sneered, his voice rising to match the screaming engine that was propelling them down the highway. "That's about me not wanting to hear some crap I know you're fixin' to tell me."

The Cadillac Eldorado seemed to lift off the roadway in apparent weightlessness as it plummeted in a furious roar toward that ever-receding, one-point perspective on the highway.

"Anthony. Anthony. You're scaring me. Please slow down!"

Anthony gradually eased off the gas pedal, allowing the car to settle into a graceful stride. They continued to ride down the Turnpike in silence for another fifteen miles. She was looking out the passenger window at nothing in particular. He was also staring straight ahead at nothing in particular.

"So what you want to talk about?" Anthony asked suddenly.

"It's OK," Rosalie muttered. "It's not worth us getting into a car wreck."

"Look, just say what's on your damned mind, all right?" his voice was unusually edgy and threatening.

"That's OK, I said. It can wait."

The engine revved up again, and the car lurched forward.

"This is crap! This is total crap!" Anthony snarled. "You started this mess. You said you had something to say. So say it, goddamn it!"

This unnerved Rosalie because until that point, Anthony's tone had always been measured and constrained, even when he was obviously upset. This attitude was new and frightening.

"I know just what the hell you're fixin' to say, so stop being such a pussy and say what's on your mind, goddamn it!"

The Cadillac's engine seemed to match the fury in Anthony's voice. Rosalie glanced at the speedometer. The car was rocketing down the highway at 110 m.p.h.

"OK. OK," she whimpered. "Just slow down, please."

She felt the car's roar gradually subside to a purr as it caught up to a convoy of tractor trailers where three lanes split off near Florence, New Jersey. They were approaching Exit 6, which would take them to Pennsylvania Turnpike. Rosalie's heart was palpitating uncontrollably, and she dropped her shaking hands into her lap.

"So what you got to say?" Anthony said, drily, still looking straight ahead at the huge trucks cautiously merging into the reduced lanes.

"Well," Rosalie began, "I was thinking that since we can't seem to get pregnant, it might make sense for now if we started to think seriously about adopting..."

Anthony's right hand suddenly shot from the steering wheel as if catapulted by a mechanical device. The back of this closed fist smashed onto Rosalie's open mouth with such force that her front teeth punctured her inner lips and sent blood gushing down her chin and onto her blouse.

His eyes never left the road nor the stream of sluggishly merging traffic, but peripherally, Anthony saw tiny beads of blood appear on the Cadillac's dashboard and instrument panel.

"You better not be messing up my goddamned car with your blood," he hissed through clenched teeth. "You hear me?"

That was Anthony's first act of violence toward her. Later, she accepted that despite the traffic, she should have found a way, somehow, to escape from the car. She could have waved her arms for help, she reasoned. She could have jumped out at the tollbooth or flagged down one of those truckers and solicited help. There was so much more she could have done at that first instance of Anthony's abuse. But she rationalized that she was in shock, and the longer she remained in the car, the more imbedded she became in fear and shame.

The fear and shame became increasingly more immobilizing over the years. Rosalie eventually subscribed to Anthony's rationale that they would have had the perfect family—the perfect life—if she had fulfilled her part of their pact. He constantly lamented that all she had to do was to present him with a son. Hell, he might have even settled for a daughter. Over the ensuing years, Anthony became violent or, at the very least, threatening, whenever reminded that he was still heirless. He was long past speculating that he had anything to do with their childlessness. It was all Rosalie's fault.

As Rosalie stepped from the plush-carpeted dining room into the kitchen, contact with the cool Italian marble tiles reminded her that she was barefooted. But she liked the feel of the cold tiles under her feet. During construction, she wanted hardwood floors throughout the house. She also wanted generous open spaces and lots of glass windows that would look out to a huge garden and spacious lawns. Anthony, however, wanted carpeting everywhere. He said he never wanted to walk on bare floors ever again. The kitchen and bathroom floors were his only concessions. Rosalie realized she must have left her slippers in the guest room after trying to reach Detective Briggs.

She had been trying to get some information about Anthony and his life in Trenton before he moved to Philadelphia. It bothered her that he didn't seem to have any history. Rosalie had no idea if she had in-laws or other relatives by marriage on the other side of the Delaware River. She, on the other hand, had a glut of relatives scattered across the Midwest. Her parents, her elder sister, Diane, and her family were all in Peoria, Illinois. They telephoned one another at least once a week, and Rosalie spent two weeks of every summer in Peoria. The family only met Anthony once, at the wedding in 1991. They all found it curious that except for an old Jewish couple, Anthony had no family or friends at the event.

And although Rosalie recounted several accounts of her family's outings, triumphs, and disasters over the years, there were no matching childhood stories about Anthony's family trips or tales of peculiar relatives. It was as if her husband's life began at nineteen, when he left Trenton for Philadelphia.

Rosalie was mildly curious at first about why he never once drove across the Benjamin Franklin Bridge to New Jersey. And for a long time, she accepted his ambiguous explanations about possibly having outstanding warrants in Trenton. But after the violence began in 1994, she became obsessed about learning what preadolescent conditions or issues might have contributed to Anthony's current violent and abusive behavior.

She spent a tremendous amount of time conducting searches for Anthony's history on her office computer. Before that, she combed the city of Trenton's telephone directory and had called every Babcock listed. During the three years of her telephone directory exploration, Rosalie actually found seventeen individuals named Anthony Babcock. However, they were either too old, too white, or too deceased. She eventually decided to check out the city's police records to pursue the outstanding-warrants theory. But an opportunity fell into her lap before she actually determined how she would access those records.

Rosalie had completed an all-day training seminar on critical thinking for the Trenton Board of Education. She stopped at Route 1 Diner on Lawrence Turnpike for a cup of coffee and a bowl of rice pudding before she left the city. Rice pudding was her favorite comfort food, and this diner served the best rice pudding. She didn't mind driving several miles out her way, especially on exhausting days, to sit peacefully in a booth and spoon down the sweet, creamy pudding slowly and deliberately.

As she pushed the empty pudding bowl away and reached for her coffee, two Trenton police officers entered the diner and walked past her to sit at the counter. One was a young blond male with twitching muscular jaws. The other was a woman, round faced and freckled, whose blond hair was tied in a bun at the back. It seemed to Rosalie that the woman would rather be watching her son play soccer than to be cooped up in a patrol car with her high-strung rookie partner. Rosalie studied them as she sipped her coffee and allowed a plan to formulate in her mind. The rookie would be of little use to her. He was too young and most likely too inexperienced to be useful. His partner, on the other hand, seemed more settled, more reflective, and in no hurry to prove herself. At this stage of his career, there was probably too much of the police academy still imbedded in him to allow him to think outside of the box. Rosalie finished her coffee, picked up the check and slid out of the booth. She walked past the couple, then she stopped and walked slowly back to stand beside the female officer.

"Excuse me," Rosalie said. "I hate to disturb you, but I wondered if you could help me with something."

She knew that she was very likely the best dressed person in the diner and that the police officers would recognize her as a professional of some kind. They would be courteous and obliging.

"Of course, ma'am," the female officer said, smiling up at Rosalie. "How can we help?"

"This might sound crazy," Rosalie said, as she stooped slightly to rest her briefcase on the floor, reading the officer's nametag as she straightened up. It read, "Chappell." "But how could I find out about an individual? I mean, if he is a bad person or not."

"Well, it depends on the situation, ma'am," Officer Chappell said. "Is this person threatening you or menacing you in any way?"

"No. No. Nothing like that," Rosalie said, smiling at the officers. "It's more for my peace of mind that I want to know what I'm dealing with."

The male officer chewed on his pastrami and Swiss cheese sandwich, not disguising his disinterest in the conversation.

"My husband is a businessman in Philadelphia," Rosalie said quickly. She wanted to hold Officer Chappell's attention for a minute. "Recently, this shady-looking guy has been showing up at his business, claiming to be a relative. My husband is a good man, but he's generous to a fault. He has been helping this man out with money, which I don't mind. But now he wants to come and to visit us at our home. I just don't trust him."

"Has he made any demands? Has he done or said anything that made you or your husband feel threatened?" Chappell asked. She sounded mildly concerned.

"No, not that I know of," Rosalie responded. "But here's the thing. Although my husband does not know this guy from a hole in the wall, he believes they might be related. That's because the guy knows a lot of my husband's family members. But he grew up here in Trenton while my husband is a Philly boy, through and through."

"So how is it you think we could help you?" Chappell asked.

"Well, I was wondering if there was some way I could find out if this guy has a criminal record or not." Rosalie said, almost whispering. Her distress felt genuine. "I know my husband. He's very trusting, and I'm afraid he's already making plans to move this man into our home."

Chappell reached into a breast pocket and pulled out a notebook. "I'm not promising anything," she said. "But I'll see what I can do." She scratched Rosalie's name and cell phone number on the notebook and asked the name of the man whose possible criminal record she intended to investigate.

"Anthony Babcock," Rosalie said. "Anthony L. Babcock."

As she backed her new 2006 Mercedes-Benz CLK-Class coupe out the parking space, Rosalie smiled broadly and popped a Patti Labelle CD into the dashboard. She quickly found the "On My Own" track and harmonized with Patti and Michael McDonald at the top of her voice as she barreled down Lawrence Turnpike toward home. She felt good.

But that feeling proved to be ephemeral, like so many other periods of elation she enjoyed over the last twelve years. She was already in bed, putting the pieces of a plan in place, when Anthony came upstairs. She felt a slight tremor of the mattress as he plopped his body onto the bed. Rosalie held her breath in the darkness. She didn't know if he would drift quietly off to sleep or if this would be one of his nights to rant and rave about her inadequacies. But she didn't have to wait long.

"I know you like to come off as so prim and proper," Anthony said. "But I was talking to the pastor the other day, and he said something very interesting about you."

"You were talking to the pastor about me? He doesn't even know me like that. What could he possibly have to say about me?"

"Well, it was more like a suggestion. Well, an opinion. He said not every woman is cut out for motherhood. He said in your case, God must know you'd be more into books and school than into raising children."

Rosalie would feel the anger rising in her in the darkness of their bedroom. Rev. Johnnie Harris didn't really know her after thirteen years in the church. Why in the world would Anthony discuss their most private concerns with him? She considered him a vain, shallow man whose literal interpretation of scripture insulted her intelligence. He was clearly threatened by intellectual and articulate people, particularly women. And she found him irritating and condescending. Although he always addressed her as Doctor Babcock, Rosalie detected an unmistakably snarky tone of condescension. He emphasized the word *doctor*, she thought, as if to imply the title was counterfeit. However, Rosalie knew he derived some vicarious pleasure from having a member with an earned doctorate among his congregation.

Rosalie considered and quickly rejected several responses to Reverend Harris's motherhood theory. Instead, she continued to stare into the darkness in silent fury.

"But here is what really got me," Anthony said. "And it kinda makes a lotta sense."

Rosalie didn't respond but wished she could fall asleep instantly and not be contaminated by any more recitations of Reverend Harris's insipid observations.

"Pastor Harris said, a lotta times when women can't get pregnant or can't carry the babies if they get pregnant is retribution for they past sinful lives."

"What?"

"Oh, that got your attention, huh?"

"Yes, it got my attention because that has to be the most asinine thing I have ever heard."

"Of course you'll say that," Anthony responded, his voice catching that gritty edge Rosalie recognized as a precursor to ferocity.

Rosalie instinctively chose silence again as her most prudent survival strategy.

"Pastor said that barrenness is most common among women in show business and with whores and prostitutes," Anthony said, slowly and deliberately, as if he were reading from a text. "He said because their morals so loose, they had to abort numerous babies. And Pastor said, because of that, their woman parts get all messed up and God have to seal up their wombs."

Rosalie felt a rush of conflicting emotions, including anger, incredulity, pity, and distress. She knew her husband was extremely street wise and a shrewd businessman. But she also knew one of his greatest vulnerabilities was an incessant search for a father figure. She noticed Anthony had a tendency to show deference to certain men. They were not necessarily older or wiser than he, but they seemed always to be men in authority over others. Whatever the reason, Anthony held Pastor Harris in unreasonably high esteem. He seemed to be on a continual quest to impress the pastor and would go out of his way to accommodate him. He would treat Pastor Harris and his colleagues to day-long golf outings, ridiculous discounts at his stores, or lavish gifts on them for no particular reason. It seemed to Rosalie that, at times, he came embarrassingly close to fawning over those men.

Rosalie knew that Anthony expected a response, but she realized she had to choose her words carefully. She anticipated that Anthony was probably on the verge of one of his explosive moods and that ignoring him could be as lethal as confronting him.

"Help me to understand what you're saying," Rosalie said, with all the composure she could muster. "Are you saying Pastor Harris is implying that I haven't been able to conceive a child because I was a whore or a prostitute before I met you?"

"I don't know if he was implying anything," Anthony spat back, the edginess increasing. "He was just explaining a biblical fact to me. And you know what? It makes a hell of a lot of sense to me."

Rosalie clenched her fists under the covers. She squeezed her eyes tightly as intermittent waves of frustration and anger washed over her. She turned toward Anthony and spoke into the darkness between them.

"Are you saying that after all you know about me, after all you know about me and my boring life before we met, you would even consider that I was promiscuous..."

"There you go with them big words again," he interrupted. "Every time we try to have a conversation, here you go with your highfalutin words. Hell, girl, everybody know you went to college. Why you can't just talk regular sometimes?"

Rosalie had the sensation of being in a runaway car with no brakes and approaching a busy intersection. She felt she had no alternative than to barrel through the crossroads and brace herself for the inevitable collision.

"OK. OK," she said, kicking off the covers and sitting up in the bed. "I don't believe you could even consider that foolishness from Reverend Harris, Anthony. You know me. You know what I was like when you met me. You know I hardly dated because I was too busy with school and working. You made fun of me because I so inhibited and wasn't *experienced*. You said yourself that I was the type of woman you considered *wife material*. So why would you even listen to that man and his crap?"

"I'll tell you why I listen to Pastor Harris," Anthony said. "First of all, he's a man of God. God speaks through him. God reveals things to him that the rest of us have no idea about, plain and simple."

"But that man is an idiot, Anthony," she pleaded. "He's an ignorant fool who is full of crap."

Without warning, Rosalie felt the back of his hand smash into her cheek. She didn't make it through the intersection. She instinctively held up an arm to ward off any blows that might come at her in the darkness and tried to jump off the bed. But Anthony reached out and grabbed her arm, fastening her to the bed.

"You see how you're always making me do things I don't want to do?" He growled. "You don't disrespect the man of God like that. Your problem is, if something ain't in one of them books of yours, then it ain't true. Well, one thing I know is true. God shut up your goddamned womb. And he made you barren, like them women in the Bible, for a reason."

Anthony was screaming by then and tightening his grip on Rosalie's arm. She nursed her throbbing cheek with her free hand, but she had stopped struggling to be free of Anthony. She had accepted that she could never free herself from Anthony, literally and figuratively, until he was ready to set her free.

"You know what I think?" he continued. "I think it was all phony, from day one. I think you were putting on this goody-goody, nice-girl act for me. The more I think about it, the more it make sense. You whore your way through college. Yeah, that's right! You wanted your education and you wanted a rich man to support you. Well, you got it, baby! You got your degrees and you got your rich man and you got your nice life."

Rosalie screamed in pain as Anthony continued to squeeze her arm. He then grabbed her by the shoulders and shook her fiercely.

"But what I got?" he screamed at her. "What I got?"

"Anthony, please," Rosalie pleaded. "You're hurting me."

"You want to know what I got? I'll tell you what I got. I got me a broke-down, barren old whore with a dried-up womb. That's what I got."

"Anthony, please stop. That's not true. You're wrong. Reverend Harris is wrong…"

"No, you're wrong! The Word of God don't lie. Pastor Harris don't lie!" he screamed as he pushed her off the bed. Rosalie remained on the floor like a pile of crumpled laundry, sobbing and heaving in the darkness. Her husband rolled over to his side of the bed and pulled the covers around him.

Rev. Johnnie Wayne Harris was the pastor of Mount Moriah Missionary Baptist Church on Broad Street. And despite the rumors, he refused to accept that Rosalie was a battered woman in an abusive relationship. That's because he knew her husband to be one of the kindest, most generous Christian men he knew. Anthony Babcock's individual financial support accounted for most of the church's computer upgrades and unsolicited repairs to the building. She knew that to complain about Anthony's chronic brutality would put Reverend Harris in an awkward position. Primarily, he would have to admit he made a mistake when he appointed Anthony Babcock to head the trustee board. But admitting to a mistake would be especially complicated for the pastor. In thirteen years, Rosalie had never heard him admit to making one.

"I don't make mistakes, although I may be a little bit off every now and again," he would say. "I am led by the Spirit to lead, and the Holy Ghost has never led me wrong."

In addition, any admission that he knew of Anthony's unpredictable, violent eruptions would cast doubt on the pastor's credentials as an excellent judge of character. Besides, both men had developed an inseparable connection over the years.

On the surface, they had few things in common. As far as Rosalie could determine, there was no common social or educational thread linking her pastor and her husband. One was a college-educated pastor who was obsessive about order and tradition, while her husband was a barely educated former street hustler turned respected entrepreneur.

Although he didn't divulge much of his past to her, Rosalie had heard the stories of Anthony's street life. He admitted that he moved to Philadelphia from Trenton in the mideighties as a teenager. He sometimes hinted that he might have been a high school dropout, but that aspect of his life, like so many others, tended to swing and sway. And from the earliest days of their relationship, Anthony's refusal to venture across the Delaware River to his home state of New Jersey puzzled her. He often mentioned his outstanding warrants in Trenton.

When they first met, Anthony loved shocking her about his life on the streets. It amused him to see her astonishment and distress when he shared bits and pieces of his former perilous life. He told her about sleeping in abandoned buildings in South Philadelphia after leaving Trenton and how he awoke once to a full-sized rat staring him in the face.

She ran out of their house one evening eleven years ago after Anthony had beaten her relentlessly for more than thirty minutes. She bolted from their second-floor bedroom, down the long driveway after Anthony took a bathroom break from the persistent beating. But before she ran out of the house, Anthony jammed Rosalie into a corner of her walk-in closet. She was naked and sweaty. He knelt in front of her, methodically slapping her in the face and punching her in the head and shoulders. He slapped her face vigorously every time she cried out in pain.

Before the beating, Rosalie was getting dressed for a reception hosted by her school district at the Haddonfield Inn in Haddonfield, New Jersey. She slipped on the outfit in her walk-in closet and stepped into the bedroom to stand in front of a full-length mirror. The ensemble featured a zipped black crocodile vest over a knee-length embroidered black-and-white skirt. She pulled it together with a three-inch-wide black patent leather belt and ankle-high black leather pumps.

Anthony walked into their bedroom as she was selecting a pair of earrings from a jewelry box on her dresser.

"Where the hell you think you going looking like that?" Anthony bellowed.

"Looking like what?" Rosalie responded, trying to restrain her irritation and anxiety.

"Looking like a goddamned hooker," he said, stepping closer to her. "You look like a cheap prostitute."

"When's the last time you saw a cheap prostitute in a four-hundred-dollar Louis Vuitton outfit?"

"Anybody could put a four-hundred-dollar dress on a two-dollar whore, and guess what?" he said, moving even closer to Rosalie. "She's still a two-dollar whore in a four-hundred-dollar dress."

"Look, Anthony, I don't want to fight with you. OK?" she responded in a much more docile voice. "I just want to go to my reception."

"Is that what y'all calling it now?" he asked, pushing up against her until she bumped into the mirror.

"C'mon, Anthony," Rosalie pleaded. "Don't start that again."

"You must think I'm some kinda chump, don't you?"

"No, Anthony. I don't think you're a chump."

"Well, you must," he said, shoving her against the mirror again. "Because don't nobody dress up like that and smell like that just to go to some reception."

"Anthony," she said, sobbing from anticipation. She knew this was foreplay to a brutal climax. They had performed this dance before. "I told you weeks ago. This is a retirement reception for some school district employees."

"See now, that's the kind of lame mess a chump would fall for," Anthony sneered, shoving Rosalie against the mirror again. "But me? Now I know when a whore is getting dressed up to do her mess."

"Anthony," Rosalie wailed, "why are you doing this? None of this is necessary."

He slapped her suddenly and hard across her face and yanked at her vest with the other hand. But the leather held and wouldn't budge. Obviously infuriated by the garment's surprising sturdiness, Anthony lunged at Rosalie and wrenched the vest by the lapels with both hands. But again, it didn't come apart. He slapped her again. Then he reached down to grab a handful of her skirt and pulled it toward him like it was the leash on an out-of-control dog. The skirt sheared apart noisily and forced Rosalie to spin around before toppling to the floor. Anthony pounced on her, planting one knee deep into her stomach while he tore furiously at the vest. He eventually managed to derail the zipper and ripped the vest off Rosalie, who continued to kick and flail her arms at him.

Anthony kept slapping her until she lost most of the feeling in her cheeks. All that was left was a throbbing numbness that tried to disguise the pain. Anthony kept yelling at her that she was no better than he was and that despite all her academic degrees, he made more money that she ever would. He let Rosalie up because he had to take a bathroom break, but by then, he had ripped every shred of the Louis Vuitton outfit off her.

As soon as she heard the sound of him urinating, Rosalie scrambled to her feet and bolted out of the room. The thick carpeting absorbed the impact of her desperate stomping as she flew down the stairs and out the front door, shoeless and in only her underwear. She continued to run down the length of their tiled driveway and out to the street, sobbing hysterically. It was dusk and already chilly, but she couldn't stop. The soles of her bare feet ached unforgivingly as they slapped against sidewalk's cold cement. She ran toward a streetlight further down the hill as if it represented a beacon of emancipation from the violence she had just escaped. But Rosalie was unaware of the black Cadillac Escalade, rolling down the hill behind her with its lights off and on the wrong side of the street.

She barely heard the thump of the front wheel as the big utility vehicle mounted the sidewalk behind her. Rosalie instinctively turned her head toward the sound, but not before Anthony's hand jutted out of the driver's window and grabbed a fistful of her hair. Anthony simultaneously gunned the engine and steered the vehicle toward the middle of the street, still holding on to Rosalie's hair. The encounter yanked her off her feet and pitched her forward to her knees. She wrapped her fingers around Anthony's outstretched arm in a futile attempt to liberate her hair from his clutch. Meanwhile, the Escalade lurched from the sidewalk to the center of the street, dragging Rosalie on her knees. But the release came only after the Escalade hit the opposite curb and stopped. She dropped to the pavement, but Anthony still held the tuft of her hair in his hand.

There was an ethereal silence for about a second. The only sound came from the SUV's deep-throated throbbing and an unrelenting chorus of cicada killers in the darkness around them. Suddenly, Rosalie's ear-piercing scream disrupted the silence. Anthony feverishly shook the bloody patch of scalp with its attached hair from his hand and sped off down the hill. No one heard her screams because all the mansions along the street were set far back on expansive acreage and hidden behind enormous hedges.

Meanwhile, the mass of hair and scalp remained in the street like road kill.

Anthony eventually returned, jammed Rosalie into the Escalade's rear seat, and drove out of Pennsylvania to a hospital in nearby Haddonfield, New Jersey. She never doubted the extent of her husband's influence after that night. It was almost a week before she was capable of any semblance of coherent thought, and it was after her care providers reduced the massive doses of pain medication. Until then, she existed in a timeless, foggy world of indefinable apparitions and hallucinations. And there was always the threat of horrendous pain lurking on the fringes of her consciousness.

But it took a while before Rosalie realized that she was on a psychiatric floor. She would hear the drone and click of electronic door locks outside her room. It was, however, the condescending attitudes of hospital personnel that convinced her that she had been placed on a suicide watch. She never found out how Anthony did it, but he had convinced hospital authorities that her injuries were self-inflicted.

That was more than eleven years ago, but the pain from that bald patch persisted. Rosalie quickly turned off her cell phone's alarm and swung her feet to the floor to feel for her slippers. She gripped the phone tightly as she shuffled in the dark toward the guest bathroom. Once there, she straightened the wig as best she could without looking directly at herself.

It was six o'clock and she didn't want to awake Anthony unnecessarily, in case he wasn't in the mood to go to church. Rosalie wasn't sure if it was his Sunday to count the tithes and offerings. And there'd be hell to pay if she woke him up on an off Sunday. His off Sundays were reserved for playing golf or sleeping in until early afternoon.

When she tiptoed into the bathroom, she made sure the light was off before opening the door. Anthony was sensitive to the slightest glow of light when he slept. She learned this from painful experience.

One night, she was sitting up in bed, frantically preparing a report to be presented at a school board meeting the following evening. Rosalie was the assistant superintendent of teaching and learning for the nearby Haddonfield, New Jersey, School District. It was regarded as one of the best school districts in the Philadelphia region. Anthony came into their bedroom from his den downstairs, abruptly turned off the overhead light and climbed into bed.

"Turn off that damned computer," he said, pulling the blanket up over his shoulders.

"OK, just give me one second," Rosalie said. "I'm just finishing this sentence."

Anthony suddenly rolled over toward her, grabbed the laptop and flung it across the room. It sailed through the darkness, its screen emitting flashes of radiance across the room like a lighthouse beacon, before crashing against a wall. Darkness and silence enveloped the room. Rosalie knew better than to attempt to retrieve her broken laptop. Instead, she got under the covers, moved closer to the edge of the bed, stared into the darkness and waited for the relief of sleep. Although she endured fifteen years of his volatile anger and abuse, Rosalie knew that in some sick way, her intense feelings of shame and degradation kept her tethered to the relationship.

She sat on the toilet and checked her messages. There was only one voice message, from a New Jersey number she didn't recognize. But instinctively, she knew this was the call she had been expecting for weeks. Rosalie pressed the phone to her ear and waited excitedly for the recording to play.

"Ms. Norfleet, this is Detective Dennis Briggs with the Trenton PD."

Rosalie had given the police officer at the Lawrence Turnpike diner her maiden name.

"Officer Chappell asked me to look into an individual," the voice continued. "And she gave me your contact information. I think I found something that might interest you."

Rosalie was shaking with excitement by the time she walked back into her room. She stretched out on top of the covers, listening to Anthony's deep breathing and stared up at the ceiling, now barely visible in the muted sunlight seeping through the window drapes.

This is happening. This is really happening. They found something. I just know it. They found something that's going to get me my freedom. Thank you, Lord! Thank you! Thank you! Thank you!

As it turned out, it was Anthony's Sunday to supervise the tithes and offering counting at Mount Moriah. So, Rosalie returned Detective Briggs's call as soon as she was alone. She managed to keep her voice calm and mildly interested as they arranged to meet the next day at the Trenton police headquarters on North Clinton Avenue.

Rosalie parked the Benz across the street from the imposing two-story redbrick building and was walking toward the entrance when she saw Detective Briggs. He was standing under an awning, his feet spread apart, just outside the entrance. She immediately and inexplicably knew who he was. His scraggy gray beard and moustache stood out against his charcoal-black face. One hand was buried deep into a black leather coat pocket. He clutched a thick accordion file under his arm while his free arm hung loosely at his side. He looked like an aging gunslinger waiting for a shootout against some unseen adversaries. Detective Briggs never shifted his gaze from her, and as she approached the building, he stepped forward with his free hand extended.

"Ms. Norfleet?" he offered.

"Ah, yes," Rosalie responded. "You must be Detective Briggs."

He apologized for meeting her in front of the building and explained that his desk was in an open squad room and he thought they needed more privacy because of the sensitive nature of their meeting.

This has to be good. This must mean something if he wants that much privacy.

Detective Briggs led Rosalie to a coffee shop down the street and pointed her to a booth near the back of the almost-deserted room. He removed his coat and threw it across the uncushioned seat and without consulting her, he walked to the counter and ordered two coffees. When he returned with the steaming black drinks, the detective sat across from her and sipped his coffee. Rosalie looked down at her cup, wondering what she would do with it since she hated coffee. When she looked up, she found Detective Briggs studying her intently and squinting as the steam from the drink floated up to his eyes. She realized that he was older than he looked initially. His short-cropped hair was peppered with patches of gray and she detected gray hairs in his eyebrows and protruding from inside his ears.

He must be single or in a bad relationship. He needs an attentive woman in his life who would pluck out those ear and nose hairs. That's something I'd be happy to do for a kind, considerate man.

Then Rosalie noticed a brown leather gun holster strap barely visible under his wrinkled navy-blue blazer. The knowledge that she was sitting less than three feet across from a pistol reminded her why she was in the coffee shop. She shifted her gaze to the thick file on the table between them.

"Officer Chappell told me you were looking for some information on an Anthony Babcock," Briggs said abruptly.

Rosalie nodded. She had become extremely apprehensive about what the files contained. Briggs patted the accordion folder with one hand as he fed the coffee into his mouth with the other. He shook his head slowly from side to side before looking directly at her.

"Officer Chappell said you and your husband were thinking of moving this person in with you."

She nodded again.

"Ma'am," Briggs hissed between his teeth, "with all due respect, that'd be a dumb-ass decision."

"Why . . ." Rosalie felt her throat constrict. Her mouth suddenly felt dry. "Why'd you say that?"

She took a sip of the hot, bitter coffee and immediately gagged and coughed a little. The detective looked at her impassively before sliding the napkin container to her. She suppressed a compelling impulse to run out of the coffee shop. Maybe she didn't want to know anything. Maybe she couldn't handle what this man was about to tell her.

"You ready to hear the rest of this, or are we leaving right now?"

"I'm sorry. Go on, please."

"OK. This Anthony Babcock y'all thinking of moving into your house, well, the only place he should be moving into is a maximum-security penitentiary."

"But why?" Rosalie whimpered. The fear in her voice was evident.

"But why?" Briggs sneered, leaning across the table and bringing his head a few inches from hers. "Because Anthony Babcock is a bad dude!"

Rosalie involuntarily took another sip of the coffee and gagged again. She grabbed a wad of napkins and held them to her face. Only her eyes, brimming with tears, were visible.

"Look, I'm not trying to scare you or anything," he said soberly and drawing back to his side of the table. "But I know this guy. He did some bad things in this city, and I've been trying to track him down for twenty years. I'm looking to retire in less than a year, and the best retirement gift for me would be to catch this dickhead and lock his sorry ass up once and for all."

"But what did he do?" Rosalie whimpered into the ball of napkins.

"What'd he do? I don't know where to start. I've been on the job for a long time and I've met all kinds of degenerates. But every time I think about this dude, I get riled up all over again."

Rosalie was sobbing hysterically by then. Whatever poise and composure she intended to bring to the meeting had dissolved. The plan was to be clever and conniving and to extract any useful information about Anthony's early life across the river. She wasn't sure just how she would use the information, but at the very least, she was hoping for some leverage. She was hoping to uncover some juvenile indiscretions that might put a dent in his current armor of Christian self-righteousness. She desperately needed some cover from Anthony's violent rages. That's why she hoped to discover a stockpile of outstanding warrants for burglaries. Even some convictions for muggings that might override New Jersey's statute of limitations would be useful. But Detective Briggs was hinting at something more ominous in Anthony's past.

Briggs told Rosalie that Anthony had been in the New Jersey child protective system from infancy. He knew this because he clandestinely gained access to Anthony's sealed juvenile delinquent records several years ago. As a ward of what used to be the state's Division of Youth and Family Services, Anthony bounced around in several foster homes across New Jersey. This was primarily because of an unpredictable, vicious streak in the child that often manifested in violent and destructive behavior.

Rosalie learned that Anthony's original last name was Pettiford until he was twelve. According to Briggs, a white middle-aged Quaker couple adopted Anthony and gave him their last name. The couple, Wade and Lauren Babcock, semiretired college professors, were intrigued with the child's violent history. The Babcocks were convinced they could repair his violent behavior with love, consistency and structure.

They were behavioral scientists who had cowritten several books and articles on social cognition and social psychology. Much of their work centered on how people managed and used information about themselves in social situations. Two years before adopting Anthony, the Babcocks began researching social attitudes among Trenton's African American residents. Their study resulted in a book and national lecture series that theorized African Americans' difficulty with establishing self-determination as US citizens. The book, *The Ethos of Victimization: The Inheritance of an Enslaved People*, attributed the turbulent history of slavery and Jim Crow to an accepted ethos of subservience and denigration. The study concluded that African Americans were destined to experience several more generations of protests and chest-thumping. The Babcocks maintained in numerous television interviews that it would take several more generations to erase the race's unconscious acceptance of discrimination and other forms of social and legal injustices.

The couple learned of Anthony from a social worker colleague during dinner one evening. The woman was depressed about the hopelessness of a young client's situation. She was convinced that the child was destined to a life of imprisonment because of his explosive behavior. The couple, whose own children were grown and gone, believed the dinner discussion was an invitation from God to save a life. They also recognized an opportunity to launch another book and lecture series. Even before meeting the child, Wade and Lauren began to speculate on the social and emotional benefits of transplanting an individual from a deprived, antagonistic environment to one that was more privileged and offered unlimited opportunities.

They read the studies and reviewed the data for several projects over the years. But those were purely for intellectual pursuits. Wade and Laurel saw a unique opportunity to become involved in a scholarly, documented project of social acculturalization. While other scientists had embraced the topic in the abstract, they envisioned their home in prestigious Villa Park and their prominent academic careers as the ideal laboratory for this experiment.

The adoption process was relatively smooth, especially after the Department of Youth and Family Services adoption officials learned of the Babcocks' prominence as social scientists. Anthony's acceptance at the prestigious Moorestown Friends School was even smoother. The Babcocks' daughter and son had been active and distinguished students at the exclusive private school. In addition, the family had been generous patrons of the institution. Consequently, the usually tedious application process seemed effortless, despite Anthony's sketchy educational history. The Babcocks took turns making the half-hour commute from Trenton to Moorestown every school day. It had been about ten years since they last made the fifty-two-mile daily roundtrip. But the anticipated academic recognition for their social experiment was too enormous to pass up.

Briggs pulled several folders from the bulky accordion file as his narration continued. He stopped abruptly to look across the table at Rosalie, who continued to sob and dab at her eyes and runny nose.

"Look," he growled, "you want to tell me what the hell is going on?"

"What do you mean?" Rosalie responded.

"Look, lady," the detective snarled, as he began to stuff file folders back into the accordion file holder. "You're not talking to a rookie! OK? People don't lose it like you're doing right now over some lowlife they don't know nothing about. You want to tell me what the hell we're doing here?"

Rosalie slowly pushed as far back as she could and allowed her body to slump into the back of the seat. She looked up at the man sitting across from her as her body involuntarily heaved several times. She looked like a caged, frightened and abused puppy in an American Society for the Prevention of Cruelty to Animals' television commercial.

"Anthony Babcock is my husband," she said between sobs. "I've been married to him for fifteen years, and my life has been a living hell for the last ten years."

Briggs put down the files, reached across the table, and patted her hand gently and briefly.

"It's OK," he muttered in the most compassionate tone he had used all morning. "It's OK."

Rosalie recounted some of the abuse she suffered over the years and even peeled back part of her wig to show Briggs the ridges of shiny scar tissue on her scalp. She revealed that he was the only person with whom she had shared any details of her married life. Rosalie admitted she had been silenced all of those years by her own deep shame.

"Most people have no idea about the level of humiliation and fear I have to live with," she said between sobs. "I have a doctorate in education. I am a respected professional who is highly recognized in my field. I try to take care of myself. I try to look good. But every morning, I wake up feeling like crap."

As Rosalie fished into her handbag for tissues and makeup, she asked Briggs what became of the adoption arrangement. He stroked the stack of files with an open palm as if it was a contented cat waiting for a treat.

"He lasted all of two years with the Babcocks before going buck wild on them," Briggs said.

According to the detective, Anthony was part of a small group of ninth-grade girls and boys in the gym playing a half-court basketball scrimmage game during their lunch hour.

"Apparently, this girl had the ball while Anthony was open and thought he had a good shot," Briggs said. "So he kept yelling at her to pass the ball, but she ignored him, took the shot instead, and missed."

Rosalie looked at him quizzically. Her look implied, "So what? What trauma could possibly ignite from kids playing a friendly game of basketball in school?"

"Well, our boy ran over to the girl, pushed her to the floor, and began kicking her in the head and torso until school staff pulled him off her."

"Oh my god!" Rosalie whispered from behind her opened hands. "But why? Why would he do that?"

"Get this," Briggs continued. "He said it was because she wouldn't pass the ball to him when he told her to. Apparently, that made him mad, and on top of that, she missed the shot."

"So what happened to that poor girl?"

"She had to be hospitalized for quite some time with head and body injuries."

"And him?" Rosalie asked. "What happened to Anthony?"

"The school expelled that little psychopath immediately, but nobody filed charges. Not a single charge."

"Really?"

"Yeah, really. I suspect that's how them rich Quakers do. I bet the Babcocks paid all the girl's medical bills and donated a truckful of money to the school."

"My lord," Rosalie sighed. "So was that the end of that?"

"Oh, hell no!" Briggs exploded. "That little lunatic was just getting started."

He said that Lauren picked up Anthony from Moorestown and was supposed to wait for her husband to get home from the Princeton campus before saying anything to Anthony. The Babcocks rarely displayed irritation, even to each other. But apparently, she couldn't contain her anger and disappointment any longer. Lauren started to reprimand Anthony immediately after stepping out of her Volvo sedan.

"She should've just left that psycho alone," Briggs said drily. "Because the minute they got in the house, that boy spun around and swung his book bag at that lady—I believe with all his strength. She took the blow to the head and fell down, unconscious."

"Oh my goodness gracious." Rosalie moaned. "Did she…"

"Did she die?" Briggs interjected. "Yeah, but not right away. But you want to know what that little monster did next?"

"I'm afraid to ask."

"This little freak commenced to kick that poor, defenseless woman on the ground like she was a dirty rag under his feet. What kind of beast does that?"

"What happened to her?"

"She ended up with broken bones in her face, broken ribs, a messed-up spleen and worst of all, brain damage. She was one of those brilliant minds that kind of wasted away in a nursing home until she died four years later. The husband retired from Princeton to take care of her, but he was never the same after the assault."

He said Wade Babcock puttered away briefly in an assisted living facility until he died quietly six months after he buried his wife.

"So you're wondering what happened to our wonder boy, right?" the detective asked.

Rosalie nodded, trying to process the enormity of her husband's path of death and destruction. She wasn't sure if she had the mental capacity to formulate thoughts into words just yet.

"Well, from age fourteen to sixteen, Anthony Babcock just vanished from Trenton. I mean, there were no formal charges against him, but we wanted to know where he was, what he was doing, and who he was hurting. He had an established pattern, even at that age. Wherever he was, people got hurt—bad. But he just vanished."

Briggs said that by 1998, Trenton police began hearing rumors of a ferocious teenager called Tony the Tiger who was robbing and brutalizing women all over the city. There were reports of mostly middle-aged women being assaulted and robbed at night in parking lots and along deserted streets. Briggs said that in a city that boasted a disproportionate number of robberies, Tony the Tiger's handiwork had become easily recognizable.

"This guy, man," Briggs said. "He always attacked women who were alone. But he wasn't satisfied with just robbing them. This punk would beat his victims in the head with a piece of lead pipe."

"And you never caught him?" Rosalie asked incredulously.

"Naw," he responded. The regret was obvious in his voice. "One of my partners said many years ago that stealth was Tony the Tiger's trademark. People didn't see him coming and after he was done, they never saw him leave. We had absolutely nothing to work with, except that my gut told me we were looking for Anthony Babcock."

"That must've been demoralizing for you as a young police officer," Rosalie offered.

"Shoot, it still is, even after all these years," Briggs said. "But you know, we almost caught a break around the Christmas season of 1989."

"Really?" Rosalie was sitting up by then and feeling excited. She was more hopeful about freedom than she had been in more than a decade.

"Yeah. We got a call late one night about a young female in distress, behind a bar on Olden Avenue in East Trenton. At first, it looked like a possible random assault. Although this was during the height of the assault robberies, I didn't connect it to Tony the Tiger at first. That's because the victim was a young black woman. The other factor that threw us off the Tiger's trail was that she was pregnant."

"Pregnant?"

"Big-time! It turned out that she was almost eight months pregnant."

"Oh my god."

"And get this," Briggs said, pausing for dramatic affect. "It turned out she was only sixteen years old."

"So how did you connect her to Anthony, er, Tony the Tiger?" Rosalie demanded. This was moving too quickly for her but she didn't want to miss a beat.

"Well, the young lady was pretty beat-up when we found her in the parking lot. It was nasty out—sleet and stuff. We found her covered in blood, huddled around a light pole, her face ripped to shreds. Some son of a bitch had used her for kicking practice."

"But she was pregnant, you said." Rosalie sobbed, raising a hand to her mouth. "What happened to her? What happened to the baby?"

"Unfortunately," Briggs said somberly, "she didn't make it."

"Oh no!" Rosalie cried. "Oh no!"

"No, she didn't make it," he repeated slowly, shaking his head.

"And the baby?" Rosalie whispered. "What happened to the baby?"

"Well, that was the only bit of silver lining to this mess," Briggs muttered. "The doctors were somehow able to save the baby."

"Oh, wow! Oh, yes! Thank you, Jesus!" Rosalie cried out as she reached out, grabbed the detective's hands between both of hers and shook them repeatedly.

Moments later, she self-consciously released his hand, wiped her eyes, and asked him about the connection to her husband.

"I rode in the ambulance with her to Saint Francis Hospital. Keep in mind, her eyes looked like ripe plumbs and her lips were bloody and so swollen, you wouldn't believe. But she kept muttering something the entire ride there."

"Were you able to understand what she was saying?"

"Yeah. Yeah. Eventually. With the siren and everything going, it wasn't until the ambulance stopped in front of the ER that I was able to understand her."

"What was she saying?" Rosalie pleaded. "What did she say?"

"She kept repeating, 'Anthony did this. Anthony did this.'"

Briggs said somberly that he had made the connection between the 1996 brutal attacks in Moorestown and in Villa Park by the time they rolled the battered girl into the ER. He said city and state police looked for Tony the Tiger all over New Jersey. They even made quiet inquiries in Philadelphia.

"But who was the girl?" Rosalie asked. "And why was she even with Tony the Tiger?"

"Her name was Latricia Sneed," Briggs said. "She lived right over there in East Trenton, not far from where she died."

"And do you have any idea why she was with him? I mean, was she just another robbery victim?"

"It's sad, really," Briggs said. "I got to know her mother pretty well after the, er, incident. Ms. Sneed was a strict church lady. She didn't play."

He speculated that Latricia started to rebel against her mother's sternness after she met Anthony. She had been a typical tenth grader who was active in school athletics, basketball in particular, and in her church youth ministry. Her mother didn't allow her to hang out, go to parties, or date. Briggs wasn't sure how or when she met Anthony, but according to her mother, Latricia changed abruptly. The once obedient and dutiful homebody became disrespectful and unmanageable. She eventually vanished.

"You see, that's the thing about Tony the Tiger," Briggs said somberly. "He could evaporate from right under your nose. And if Latricia was with him, then she became as invisible as he was."

He reasoned that the excitement of stealing and hiding out with Anthony must have diminished considerably, particularly after she became pregnant. He said there was evidence that the couple lived in abandoned warehouses and boarded-up buildings for months.

"You know what I think?" Briggs asked rhetorically. "I think because the poor girl was pregnant, she was literally sick, tired, and cold. She just wanted to go home."

The detective speculated that Latricia had left Anthony and was sneaking back home. He must have caught up with her only a few blocks from her mother's home.

"So this is the bottom line for me," Briggs said gravely. "I can't speak for nobody else. But I feel like that little girl didn't have to die like that. And because there's no statute of limitation on murder, I decided a long time ago that I was going to do all I could to get justice for Latricia. That's why I'm still carrying this."

Briggs made a fist with his right hand to show Rosalie a half-inch tattoo of "LS" within overlapping circles. The circle, he said, represented handcuffs. He told her that he would seriously consider retirement after Latricia's murderer was arrested and convicted. Rosalie touched the tattoo briefly and brushed away a tear.

"So tell me about the baby," Rosalie whispered. "What happened to the baby?"

Briggs held up a forefinger, slid out of the booth, and went to the counter to order two more coffees. Rosalie discerned that it was a sensitive moment for him, and he probably did not relish showing his emotions. She waited impatiently for him to return but was distinctly apprehensive about what she might learn. Her best guess was that the detective didn't know what had become of Latricia's baby. However, she couldn't dismiss a potentially ironic possibility that floated across her consciousness.

Anthony had waged continuous, vicious physical and emotional guerrilla warfare against her for fifteen years because she never produced the son he craved so intensely. He fabricated his vehemence around her inability to conceive an heir to his legacy. And it troubled her tremendously that a possible biological malfunction, over which she was powerless, had been the nucleus of his rage for so long. And one of the casualties of that protracted combat was her inability to recall the early sensations of love and peace in her marriage.

Rosalie waited until the detective settled himself in the booth and after they had both sipped their coffees to look directly across the table at him.

"Well?" she asked, with all the composure she could muster. "Do you know what happened to the little boy?"

"As a matter of fact, I do," Briggs said, allowing a hint of a smile before taking another sip of his coffee. "I have stayed in touch with Ms. Sneed over the years. I mean, I couldn't forget her. To me, she wasn't just another single mom who had to bury her child. She now had to raise a grandson who was born premature. Let me tell you. That boy stayed sick. And Ms. Sneed, she worked housekeeping in a hotel, cleaning rooms for chump change. But she took care of that boy with hardly no help from nobody."

Briggs told her that he and his colleagues, especially those who remembered the case, kept an eye on Levi Sneed, mostly from a distance. He said the child was a late bloomer, small for his age, and too sickly to play basketball and stickball in the street with neighborhood kids. But by age twelve, Levi hit a brisk growth streak. He had grown into a tall, lanky and agile young man. Briggs said he remembered him being a standout basketball player in several outdoor tournaments.

"But for all that," he said, "Levi never got into nothing bad. His grandmother stayed on him. I mean, she let him do all the normal things, you know. Play ball. He took music lessons. Things like that. But she didn't let him hang out or none of that. Lots of times, I'd see him walking home alone, carrying his guitar case. He's a real nice young man."

And before Rosalie could ask, Briggs told her Levi was a second-year student at Mercer Community College, studying business management. He added that Levi had always been an excellent student and had been accepted to several Ivy League colleges. But without offers of full scholarships, the community college turned out to be his only option. Briggs said Levi's grandmother was a private woman, especially after her daughter's death. But she explored every resource at her disposal, in and around Trenton, to fund Levi's college education.

"It was kind of sad, really," Briggs said. "Ms. Sneed went to Black Churches, white churches. She went to the NAACP. I mean, that woman pounded on some doors in this city. She went wherever she could to get grants, scholarships, anything so that boy could go to Princeton or Rutgers. You have to remember, she always kept to herself, so it wasn't easy for her to go asking for favors like that. She would do anything for that boy. He's her life."

But in the end, and despite the best efforts of most of the colleges, there wasn't enough financial aid, grants, and community scholarships to logically fund a four-year college degree. And Roberta Sneed extracted a promise from her grandson that under no circumstances would they allow themselves to be buried under hundreds of thousands of dollars of student loan debt.

"I really don't know why," Briggs said, smiling and shaking his head. "But that woman was dead set against owing the banks nothing. Couple of times, me, my wife, other people tried to talk her into applying for college loans. Naw, man, she wasn't having it."

"So because of her pride or her aversion to banks," Rosalie said, clearly exasperated, "this young man, who, from what you say, could have a brilliant future, ends up in some community college?"

"Hey, hey," the detective pleaded, holding up his hands in protest. "Don't go killing the messenger now. I'm just telling you how it is, OK? Yes, the boy's bright. But that doesn't change the fact that his grandmother is an underpaid hotel worker who can't afford to give the boy an Ivy League education. Period."

"Well, I'm sorry, but screw that!" Rosalie pounded the table, causing some of her untouched coffee to spill over the rim of the paper cup. "That boy is going to Princeton, Columbia, or any damned school he chooses. And you can take that to the bank."

Rosalie was surprised by her outburst and instantly regretful for the shock she saw registered on the detective's face. She instinctively began cleaning up the spilled coffee with a napkin and stopped when she felt hot tears sliding down her cheeks. Rosalie wiped her eyes and cheeks with the damp napkin before twisting it in her lap. She looked down at her hands for a moment before looking up and away to the other side of the room. It was as if she needed a safe resting place for her eyes. Briggs looked at her with a mixture of confusion and concern.

"I know. I know. It's crazy," Rosalie said, attempting to smile. "I didn't even know the child existed twenty minutes ago. And now I'm upset because he can't afford to attend the college of his choice. And it absolutely infuriates me that my husband, who might be his father, can more than afford to send ten young people like Levi to any damned school in the country."

Rosalie was now in full wailing mode. Meanwhile, Briggs continued to sit, looking impassively across the table at her. The coffee shop was empty, except for two people behind the counter, so he didn't have to worry about attracting too much attention. He had never developed a tolerance for hysterics, but he was willing to ride this episode out. Briggs was convinced that his two decades of agonizing over Tony the Tiger was about over. Despite some personal and professional accomplishments, he never shook off the daily anger and impotence he felt over letting Anthony Babcock slip away. So he was willing to put up with a little sniveling from this woman who said she was indeed married to his nemesis. He was about to grab a tiger by the tail.

"Well, I'll tell you one thing, Detective Briggs," Rosalie said, wiping her eyes and stepping out of the booth. "When I'm done with this, that poor young man will have the best education money can buy. You can take that to the bank. And you know what else you can take to the bank?"

"I can't wait to hear, Mrs. Babcock," Briggs said, reaching for his leather coat. "What else can I take to the bank?"

"I'm going to give you your Tony the Tiger for Christmas, all wrapped up in a big red bow. You can believe that!"

As he held the door for her to climb into her car, Briggs saw the steely determination of a resolute woman. She had abandoned the weepy, anguished look in the coffee shop. He allowed a feeling of warm exhilaration to envelope him as he replayed their parting understanding. They agreed that Rosalie would devise a way to get her husband into New Jersey where Briggs and his law enforcement colleagues would arrest him. There was no doubt in his mind that she meant every one of her parting words. "When I call you, just come and pick him up."

Rosalie rifled through her CD collection in the glove compartment and stuck Anita Baker's 1983 *The Songstress* album into the player. She selected "No More Tears" as soon as the machine swallowed the disk, waved goodbye to the detective and pulled the Benz into the midafternoon traffic.

A gleaming black Range Rover Classic greeted Rosalie as she pulled into the driveway. Anthony was normally fastidious about backing the vehicles into their three-car garage. But she supposed he wanted to make sure she didn't miss his latest possession. She found him sitting at the kitchen table, pouring over the owner's manual and looking like a kid with a new bicycle. Anthony was unusually buoyant. His effervescent congeniality made Rosalie weirdly uncomfortable. He insisted on taking her outside for a guided tour of the vehicle before she could climb out of her coat. Although she was mildly amused by his excitement, Rosalie wondered about his elation over this particular SUV. It wasn't like it was his first new car. He owned a slew of them over the years, different makes and models, and made an issue of replacing them every three years. But she didn't have to wait long to find out why he was so bubbly about the Range Rover.

"Did you know the queen of England has this same model?" Anthony gushed as he led her to the car. "They designed it especially for her to go fox hunting and driving in the country."

He opened the passenger door and gestured her in. The new-car smell blanketed her immediately. As she climbed up into the front seat, Anthony raced around the car and got behind the wheel but made no attempt to start it. Instead, he pointed to various features while looking at her for some sign of approval. Rosalie actually felt pity for her husband because he had no authentic friends with whom he could share this moment. She knew he would eventually unveil his latest toy to his pastor and to his golf acquaintances. And she understood how much he really craved some genuine admiration at that moment. But sadly, Rosalie did not have it. The best she could offer was an artificial smile and the occasional perfunctory nod.

"The sales guy told me this is the exact model they customized for the Popemobile," he said breathlessly.

Rosalie realized that Anthony was laboring hard for some indication of genuine admiration for his acquisition. So she cut to the chase and gave him the opening he really needed.

"So what did you pay for all this?" she asked, patting the leather dashboard.

"You don't want to know," Anthony replied, grinning at her.

"No, really," she responded. "Maybe I'll get me a matching one."

His smile vanished immediately, and he looked her with a trace of scorn.

"I don't think so," he spat at her. "This baby cost me one hundred and thirty thousand grand. How you fixing to match that?"

Anthony abruptly opened the door, jumped out of the Range Rover, and walked briskly up the driveway to the house.

The following Sunday, Rosalie awoke to the rhythmic sound of ice flinging against the bedroom window. Because it was still dark out, she wondered if she should remain in bed or get ready for church. It was Anthony's turn to oversee counting the tithes and offerings, and she knew he wanted to arrive early enough to park his new Range Rover Classic next to the pastor's space. She was about to settle back under the covers when she jolted herself erect and threw off the sheets.

"Thank you, Jesus!" she whispered. "Thank you, Lord!"

Rosalie unplugged her cell phone before going to the bathroom. She then pulled on some sweatpants before grabbing a coat downstairs. She quietly picked up Anthony's car keys from the kitchen key rack and headed for the garage. Rosalie was breathing so heavily that she had to stop and compose herself before climbing into the Range Rover. There was no chance Anthony could hear anything from their bedroom because the garage was on the other side of the sprawling house. Rosalie eased the SUV out of the garage, put it in neutral, and allowed it to roll down the driveway and into the street. She then drove around the block and parked on the hill, where she had a clear view of their driveway.

The phone rang in their bedroom several times before it went to the recorder. Rosalie called the number three times before Anthony picked up the phone.

"Yeah. Who's this?" he sounded groggy and angry.

"It's me." Rosalie didn't have to fake her nervousness. She held the phone with both hands because they shook so violently.

"What the hell you're doing calling the house?" he roared into the phone. "Where the hell are you?"

"Something happened," she cried. "Something happened, and I'm stuck out here."

"Something happened? Something happened? Like what? Where the hell are you anyway?" Anthony shrieked.

"I had an accident on Lawrence Turnpike . . ."

"Lawrence Turnpike in Trenton? What the hell you doing in Trenton at five thirty in the goddamned morning?"

"I have a presentation in Harrisburg early Monday morning and I forgot all my notes in my office . . ."

"What the hell?" Anthony screamed. "You in Jersey? You must be out of your damned mind. You on your own, you crazy bitch!"

"I'm sorry. I'm sorry," Rosalie pleaded. "I panicked. I couldn't sleep. So I decided to go get them. The ice didn't get really bad until I started back. I'm really sorry."

"You sorry? You sorry? You think you sorry now. You gonna know sorry when your ass gets here."

The phone went dead. Rosalie redialed several times without any response. She then called his cell phone.

"What you want now?" he snarled. "I ain't saying it again. You on your own. I don't give a shit how you getting back here because I ain't going to Jersey!"

"Oh, I forgot to tell you," she interrupted. "I took the Range Rover. It skidded off the road into a ditch."

"What?" Anthony bellowed. "What you say, bitch? You took what?"

Rosalie didn't respond. She just smiled and held the phone aloft until the squawking on the other end ceased.

"What did you say, Anthony?" she asked when she replaced the phone to her ear. "I didn't hear you."

"I said, where are you?"

"The car is off the road across from the Route 1 Diner on Lawrence Turnpike, just outside Trenton. I'm sitting inside."

Rosalie abruptly ended the call and immediately dialed Detective Briggs' number.

"A tiger will be prowling around a certain diner on Lawrence Turnpike in about an hour," she said melodiously. "You don't want to miss him."

Rosalie sat motionless in the Range Rover until she saw the lights of her car pierce into the icy darkness. She held her breath as Anthony drove it down the driveway. She watched it turn down the street and didn't exhale until the twin blobs of red taillights disappeared down the hill.

###

THE FLAMBOYANT USHER

Francine loved being an usher.

But for reasons that perplexed her, most people didn't believe she was usher material.

She, however, sincerely believed she was divinely called to the ministry. As far as she was concerned, her call to ushering was as valid as her pastor's call to preaching. That's because it often took the intervention of the Holy Spirit to deal with some of the folks who gave her serious attitude as they walked through the doors on Sunday mornings. Some of them blamed her for the changing demographics of their church in Scranton, Pennsylvania.

It seemed that for a good while, God kept sending an awful lot of weird folk to Redeeming Blood Baptist Church. At least that's what some church members muttered among themselves. Some wondered why, of all the churches in Scranton, Pennsylvania, *those people* kept showing up at Redeeming Blood.

"Is that Francine girl with the nose ring and that thing sticking out of her tongue. I can't stand to look at it," Mother Essie Mae Bowden whispered to her crony Deaconess Helena Monfere during a Sunday service. "You ever noticed that ever since she join Redeeming Blood, all *those people* start showing up?"

"You know," Deaconess Monfere replied, "you're not the first person to mention it. You right. Is true. *Those people* never came here until Francine join and start ushering."

"I can't say I'm surprised, though," Mother Bowden whispered behind her fan. "Seeing where she hang out."

This was getting good. It was more than Deaconess Monfere expected.

"Where she hanging out?" she asked excitedly, just above a whisper.

"Well, me and Duncan saw her on West Olive Street one time, talking to some of *those people* in front of the Keystone Rescue Mission," Mother

Bowden said. "At first, I didn't think too much about it. But another time, we went to drop off some stuff at the place . . . what you call it . . . Angel's Attic or something like that. And there she is, packing food in bags . . ."

"What's that?"

"Angel's Attic? Is a United Neighborhood Center place, right there on Olive Street. It's where homeless and poor people go to get food and clothes and stuff."

"She packing food for herself?"

"No. I think she either working there or she volunteering or something."

"She see y'all?"

"Naw. Naw. I don't think so. But I'm sure that's where she be seeing all *those people*. I bet she be inviting them to come to Redeeming Blood."

"Uh, uh, uh. That ain't right."

And as if to reinforce their point, there was a couple who almost disrupted the service last Palm Sunday. They pushed against the vestibule double doors so violently that Francine and Estelle Bey-Herring were almost thrown to the floor. Francine and Estelle were at their posts on either side of the doors that Sunday, just inside the sanctuary. Suddenly, the heavy mahogany-and-smoked-glass doors flew open, simultaneously knocking them off their feet. Estelle stumbled to her knees.

The man looked like a big black beer keg—squat, thick, and heavy. His companion, on the other hand, was emaciated and ghostly. Her bulging, bloodshot eyes seemed to be looking everywhere but seeing nothing. A top rack of ill-fitting false teeth seemed poised to drop from her mouth at any second. They both reeked of stale alcohol and evaporated sweat. An enormous fire-breathing golden dragon emblazed on the front of the man's black silk shirt seemed ready to lunge every time his big belly expanded. The woman's lime-green pants suit was wrinkled and stained. The spaghetti strap had slipped off one shoulder, revealing a bony back and protruding collarbones. They could have been on a liquor run from whatever all-night party they had attended and couldn't find their way back.

The couple staggered up the center aisle toward the pulpit area where the deacons were just winding up the devotion period. The approximately two hundred people in the sanctuary stared at them in startled silence as they swayed closer to the pulpit.

"Hey, what y'all looking at?" The man growled. "Today Palm Sunday, ain't it?"

"Yeah, it sure is!" the skinny woman responded. She wobbled slightly and grabbed her partner's arm to steady herself. "It sure is! My baby boy told me last night. He said, 'Momma, I'm going to church tomorrow, and

I'm gonna get you a palm.' But I told him, I said, 'Don't you never mind, sugar. Momma's gonna get her own damn palm.' So I come to get my palm. Where my palm at?"

The man scanned the congregation slowly. His face was puffy and gray; his eyes moist and red. He threw his arms around the woman in a feigned show of gallantry. But it was obvious that he needed her body's support if he were to remain on his own feet.

"So lookey here. Where the palms at?" he asked, attempting to swivel his large head without toppling over. "If my lady wants a palm, then she getting a palm. That's all I got to say 'bout it."

He fished into a hip pocket with his free hand and pulled out a battered wallet.

"Don't worry 'bout nothing," he sputtered, holding up the wallet. "I got money. I keeps me some money. How much for the damn palms anyway?"

Two of the eight elderly deacons conducting devotions stood together near the pulpit area, looking bewildered. They appeared ready to race one another to the door if the drunk couple so much as looked in their direction. The other deacons found seats on the first pew and seemed to ignore the activities at the center aisle. The deacons were obviously stumped, especially since the pastor, who was still in his study, wasn't there to tell them what to do.

That's when Francine strode up the aisle, her starched white ushers uniform snapping with every step. She approached the couple, holding two green palm leaves aloft. Her smile broadened as she approached them. There was no trace of impatience or annoyance in her demeanor. Estelle, meanwhile, who resumed her position at the door, brushed off her knees. She continued to scowl menacingly at the couple who had knocked her to the ground. She had emphatically declined Francine's suggestion that they take a few palms up to the couple.

"These are for you," Francine said sweetly, extending the palm leaves to the woman. "I know y'all probably came a long way to get them, and I'm sure you have to get right back."

The woman reached out and grabbed the leaves from Francine's white-gloved hand. She held the long, slender palm leaves as she might have once carried a wedding bouquet. She then attempted a dainty curtsy. But she toppled instead, headfirst to the floor, dragging her companion down with her.

Francine was the quintessential usher who effortlessly demonstrated genuine love and compassion. And the children adored her. Most Sundays after church, youngsters would badger their parents for permission to go off with Sister Francine. She would cram as many of them as she could into her little yellow-and-black Mini Cooper and speed off to some spontaneous adventure. Her favorite destinations in the summer months were the Houdini Museum on North Main Avenue, Nay Aug Park, or McDade Park.

And although she was twenty-four years old, Francine still had a childlike fascination with magic and parks. Last year, she bought a seventy-five-dollar family season pass for the summer for Nay Aug Park. That's because, like the children, she couldn't seem to get enough of the rides and waterslide. She loved the Sunday afternoon outings with the kids because they seemed to get the same thrill every time they crossed the covered footbridge over the Roaring Brook. There was that same satisfaction every time she took a group of church children to the David Wenzel Treehouse and watch them discover some new wonder in the gorge that rose 150 feet above them.

The children loved Francine with about the same intensity that most Redeeming Blood adults hated her. They hated her for not fitting in and for her indifference about conventional church attire. But more than anything else, they despised her for not showing the slightest inclination to blend in, even a little bit.

They knew this because she wore Chuck Taylor Converse sneakers everywhere and with everything. She possessed every conceivable style and color and sometimes wore a different color sneaker on each foot—but never when she was ushering. Francine always wore classic white high-top Chucks to match her white usher's uniform. That, along with her lavish assortment of fingernail polish and her head full of bushy twists, generated a tremendous amount of contempt from the church's traditionalist majority.

Immediately following the Palm Sunday incident, a contingent of the church's unofficial fashion and decorum police approached Angela Randolph—a longtime head of the usher board. They gathered around her in a tight circle at the back of the sanctuary as she was about to replace discarded fans she had picked up in the pews. The concerned committee wanted to know how long they had to tolerate Francine as an usher.

"Look, if it was up to me," she pleaded, "that young lady wouldn't never be part of the usher board."

"Well, who else it's up to? You in charge of the ushers, ain't you?" Trustee Gladys Ruffin asked.

"It's true. You're right," Usher Randolph responded. "But I can't go over the pastor's head."

"That's what you always say, and we keep telling you, we willing to go in with you to talk to Pastor. But you never do nothing," interjected Mother Bowden. "You know good and well that if you stand up strong to Pastor, he'll back down."

"Please don't tell me you got her ushering next Sunday," Trustee Ruffin said. "You realize next Sunday is Easter Sunday, don't you?"

"No, it ain't her turn to usher until the third Sunday in April. I make sure of that," Head Usher Randolph said proudly. "We always have all kinda visitors and strangers coming here for Easter. I'm not trying to have Ms. Nappyhead-Gypsy-Hippie be the first thing they see when they come up in here."

"Good!" Mother Bowden said. "And remember, soon as you want me to go with you to talk to Pastor, just let me know."

The truth was that Head Usher Randolph actually liked Francine. And although the young woman chose to look different and be different, she greatly admired her fellow usher's compassion and selflessness. She secretly wished she possessed Francine's gregarious nature and her ability to interact so effortlessly with society's rejects. She often observed with amazement how easily Francine would make the most introverted visitors respond to her or how she never hesitated to shake hands and sometimes even hug obviously destitute people who ventured up Redeeming Blood's front steps. But being well versed in church politics, Head Usher Randolph realized the expediency of criticizing Francine's appearance to the church leadership. As a matter of fact, it was she who created the clandestine nickname Ms. Nappyhead-Gypsy-Hippie.

And through it all, Francine appeared oblivious to the furor her nonconformist appearance generated at Redeeming Blood Baptist Church. She always sat up front in the second or third row of pews when she wasn't serving as an usher. Much to the chagrin of the fashion and decorum police, she was usually the first on her feet, clapping with the music or encouraging the preacher.

The rank and file traditionalists had long since given up on speculating how Francine would show out in church on any Sunday. However, the following Sunday was Easter—the highest and holiest of all Christian celebrations. That's when, next to Mother's Day, Black Churches experience the year's highest attendance. In anticipation of the increased turnout, the faithful scrub, dust, polish, and paint the sanctuaries.

It is the day when fathers and sons sport day-old haircuts. The day also features little boys fidgeting in new two- or three-piece suits, usually two sizes too large. It's on Easter Sunday that children get their annual reinforcement of what constitutes proper church attire. The young boys wear clip-on ties that rarely make it back home because after a while, the alligator clips lose their bite into the unyielding polyester shirt collars.

Then there are the little girls who survive agonizing hours of hair straightening or braiding, only to have them hidden under what mothers and grandmothers perceive to be delightful pink or yellow Easter bonnets. But they had an advantage over their brothers who had to settle for the shapeless Easter suits they were expected to grow into. The girls had inexhaustible choices of pink or yellow dresses that fit perfectly. And again, unlike their brothers, they had the gift of choice.

But Easter Sunday really belongs to those church women of a certain age. Most of them possess an uncanny fashion sense that gives them license to unleash a tradition of style and glamor that's unique to the Black Church. And it is on Easter Sunday morning when they unveil this cavalcade of fashion. It is a spectacle of allure and elegance in which the conventional hallmarks of beauty, such as slenderness and fashion-model attractiveness, become irrelevant.

In this unofficial fashion pageant, the contestants are allowed to be fashionably late—as long as they can strut their stuff. There is an unmistakable Easter Sunday strut that's nothing like the swaying sashay perfected by conventional runway models. The Easter Sunday strut is an unhurried but deliberate saunter to a predetermined point along the center aisle. It's critical to know the precise spot where she will stop and turn slowly but purposefully into her seat. It's like an airplane pilot knowing just where his wheels will hit the approaching runway. But the entire impact of her entrance would be lost if she misses her target, is denied a seat, and has to scrounge around for somewhere to sit. The entrance is everything.

That Sunday, there was a buzz and the muted rustle of fabric as most heads in the sanctuary craned around in brazen curiosity. It was Squeaky Whittaker and his girlfriend Gwen making their annual Easter Sunday appearance. Several years ago, he bought and sold welfare food stamps at the back room of his barbershop on Farr Street in the downtown section. But in the last decade, Squeaky had morphed into a respectable slumlord.

He and Gwen had come to reclaim their standing as the most distinguished Easter Sunday couple. According to the general consensus, they lost last year to Connie and Ephraim McMillian. However, rumor had it that the McMillians skipped Redeeming Blood this year and were looking for a larger church at which they could dress to impress.

By all accounts, Connie and Ephraim would have had a run for their money this year. That's because Squeaky strutted down the aisle wearing a knee-length, contoured, flamingo-pink jacket with matching pants. He sported a double-knotted wide solid-pink tie over a canary-yellow shirt and yellow, patent leather, slip-on shoes. He topped it off with a pink fedora hat that remained on his head throughout the service. There wasn't one person in the church who was brave enough to suggest that Squeaky remove his hat.

And there was Gwen, about a full step behind Squeaky. She, like everyone else, knew this Easter Sunday church appearance was all about Squeaky. So, she didn't mind playing runner-up to her man's swag. It was in her best interest to allow him the opportunity to present himself on Easter Sunday in all his ghetto fabulousness. That's because he was most generous to her whenever she reassured him that he was the king of the ball. She realized how important his Easter show out was to him. She already knew what she would say to him on the ride home.

"Squeaky, you was squeaky clean again today, baby."

It never got tired, no matter how many times she said it.

And Gwen was a portrait of matching, blazing pinkness. She wore a tight pink latex-like dress that shimmered with each step. It could have been mistaken for a water-drenched bodysuit. It was clear the dress revealed too much of Gwen's hefty thighs to please Mother Bowden. But no one was about to say anything to Squeaky's woman. The fashion police and their deputies just stared in disapproving silence. With her above-the-calf, pink stiletto boots and pink bowler hat securely fastened to her pink-highlighted wig, Gwen strut up the aisle behind Squeaky toward the pulpit area. They then turned and walked slowly and purposefully back down the center aisle to find seats at the rear of the sanctuary under the balcony. The bizarre procession was startling only to newcomers. Longtimers had seen different variations of this Easter parade over the years.

Then Pastor Eric D. Kidd emerged from his study, and the heads in the sanctuary swiveled away from Squeaky and Gwen toward the pulpit. It was as if he had waited in his office until the heads-up came that Squeaky and his lady had settled into their seats. He climbed the two stairs to the platform followed by three robed associate ministers. Some members had complained that unrobed ministers on the pulpit seemed unsightly. Even if all the associates did was sit passively throughout the service, these members wanted their pulpit decked with somberly robed ministers.

So Pastor Kidd, who valued conflict avoidance above everything else, decreed that his associate ministers would wear robes on the pulpit. As a result, the three young men usually sat there in glassy-eyed boredom. That's when they were not acting out feigned enthusiasm at some oft-repeated preaching cliché coming from the podium. The people didn't mind having their ministers become pulpit ornaments. They liked that it looked dignified.

The pastor was about to rise from his pulpit chair to offer the invocation when Francine pushed through the great glass doors in the vestibule and rushed up the center aisle. She was heading toward her usual seat in the second row, right. She had breathlessly explained to the greeters as she rushed up the front steps that she was on Olive Street, looking for one of her United Neighborhood Center clients. She had arranged to meet a homeless young woman in front of the center, buy her breakfast, and bring her to church. Francine spent forty-five minutes looking for the young woman before reluctantly giving up the search and rushing to Redeeming Blood.

Although she was oblivious to the commotion her entrance created, her appearance generated more disruption than Squeaky and Gwen's. She wore a pair of black tights under a loose-fitting tie-dye, yellow, cotton dress. Great swirling patterns of green and red circles within circles covered the dress. She had tied a green, yellow, and red scarf around her head, from which scores of her tightly wound minilocks protruded. And on her feet were her iconic high-top Chucks. Only this time, apparently in the spirit of Easter, Francine wore one red and one green sneaker.

She scurried to her usual seat—second row, right—feeling tremendously relieved. Although she was late, someone held her seat. It was obvious because there was a generous space at the end of the pew. But as she approached the pew, the person occupying the seat next to the space suddenly slid over to the empty spot.

It's all good, Francine thought. *It happens all the time. Some people love their aisle seat.*

So, she attempted to move into the space the person created when she slid over. But that wasn't to be. The woman shifted back to the open space.

Oh, this is getting serious, Francine thought.

Until this point, Francine hadn't looked at the woman because she had been facing toward the pulpit and hadn't bothered to look back. She had fully expected to be seated in short order. Francine then turned around to see the scowling face of Erica Shaw, Deaconess Monfere's daughter.

"Excuse me! Excuse me!" Erica Shaw hissed. "You can't sit here."

"I can't sit here?" Francine asked, clearly puzzled. "There's enough room. I don't understand why I can't sit here."

"Well, I'm telling you, you can't sit here today!" Erica Shaw said defiantly and more than a few decibels above a whisper.

She planted two plump heavily bejeweled hands on the pew cushion on either side of her portly body. Her eyes dared Francine to attempt sitting on her hands. Pastor Kidd was immediately aware of the brewing conflict, like most people seated in the church's front section. But he chose to ignore it. Instead, he folded his arms, placed an index finger across his lips, and nodded his head mechanically. He looked like a toy, a bobbing-head dog that people used to glue to their dashboards. He was either waiting for the issue to resolve itself or for some divine intervention. But it was clear that he was not going to get embroiled in a seat conflict between his head deacon's married daughter and Francine. He liked Francine and her free spirit, but not enough to jeopardize his tenuous relationship with the church's leadership.

Francine reluctantly eased out of the pew, stood in the aisle for a moment before retreating to a pew, further back on the other side. She thought she had seen a space back there. But by the time she arrived, the space had mysteriously vanished. Francine tried three more times to find a seat next to people she knew, people with whom she thought she had, if not relationships, at least some rapport. But those individuals closed the gap in every case.

She stood like a lost puppy on the red-carpeted aisle for several seconds—first, turning one way and then the other. She realized by then she had attracted the attention of the entire sanctuary. Pastor Kidd read the look of bewilderment and betrayal on Francine's face. She looked like a little, unwanted, and friendless girl at a party. But he reasoned, he couldn't force people to be accommodating to Francine. After all, she brought this on herself. Why did she insist on being so strange anyway? He already stuck his neck out for her several times by not responding to the many requests to remove her from the usher board.

After a while, Francine turned to look at the pastor and failing to catch his eye, she slowly walked out the doors to the vestibule and up the stairs to the balcony. Pastor Kidd didn't arise to do the invocation until the sanctuary doors closed behind her.

He was surprised to see Francine standing outside his office after the service. He was sure the humiliation she must have felt that morning would drive her from Redeeming Blood. He didn't think he would ever see her at the church again and that saddened him. So he was actually relieved to see her standing there. He called her into the office after he took off his robe. Pastor Kidd started to sit behind the large ornate but immaculately clean desk but chose instead one of the pair of overstuffed brown leather chairs. He motioned Francine to the other chair, sat back, crossed his legs, and nodded at her.

"I think I know why you came to see me," Pastor Kidd said softly, almost apologetically. "It's about that incident in the sanctuary, isn't it?"

"Yes, Pastor," Francine replied.

"I know. I know," he said. "I was very distressed. Very distressed."

"Well, to tell you the truth, Pastor," Francine said, shaking her head sadly, "it didn't look like you or anybody saw what was happening. And if they saw, well, they sure didn't care."

"You're right. You're so right." he responded, his voice soothing and drenched with compassion. It was the tone he invoked for hospital visits and bereaved relatives.

"But I don't understand why nobody offered me a seat or tried to help me," Francine said, the pain in her voice palpable. "Not even you, Pastor."

It was not accusatory. She seemed authentically bewildered.

Pastor Kidd continued to nod his head in his iconic mechanical movement. He then leaned forward ever so slightly, one hand cupping his chin, the other stroking the smooth leather of the chair's armrest. It was as if he were substituting the armrest for Francine's hand. The gesture gave her some allegorical reassurance.

"Francine," he said, almost in a whisper. "I apologize for not standing up for you this morning. But you have to understand my position here as the pastor of this church."

"I'm not understanding…"

"Let me finish," he interrupted. "I feel bad admitting this but I'm what you call a caretaker pastor."

He held up two fingers on each hand to indicate air quotes.

"What's a caretaker pastor? How's that different from a regular pastor?"

"You see, when I took this position, I knew I wasn't going to change anything. I already knew who was in charge and who had the power. A few of my predecessors came in here all bright-eyed and bushy-tailed, thinking they were going to shake things up. They're gone! One or two of them came here right out of seminary, their heads full of all kinds of progressive and innovative ideas. They didn't last as long as a snowflake in hell. You see what I'm saying?"

Francine's confusion was clear. She frowned deeply, shook her head slowly from side to side, and looked at Pastor Kidd through squinted eyes.

"I'm not understanding this," she said. "Isn't the pastor the leader of the church? Isn't the pastor supposed to prayerfully make whatever changes are necessary under the direction of the Holy Ghost?"

"Well, usually, yes," Pastor Kidd answered. "Under normal conditions, the pastor should be the spiritual leader of the church. But there's nothing normal here at Redeeming Blood. There are three or four families that have always controlled everything that goes on in this church. You've been here long enough. I'm surprised you don't recognize them. They have been running things here for generations."

"Wait a minute. Hold up," Francine interjected, sitting up in her chair. "Are you telling me this isn't God's church? This is their church?"

"Well, that's how they see it and that's how their parents before them saw it. These people are no joke. They're serious about running this church their way. Check this out. A few years ago and a few pastors back, this young seminarian decided he was going to preach a series of sermons on, I think it was the compassion of Christ. I heard they left him alone for about two sermons. Then he started getting deep. He started preaching about how the church needed to be 'doers of the Word, not just hearers of the Word.' He was coming up with all kinds of suggestions about how church members could be more compassionate to one another and to the community."

"That sounds good," Francine said. "What's wrong with that?"

Pastor Kidd leaned back in his chair and crossed his legs. He was obviously more relaxed and enjoying the reception his story was receiving.

"What's wrong with that? I'll tell you what's wrong with that," he said. "They didn't like having to shift from the abstract to the application. They didn't mind listening to the sermons. But when there was a requirement for them to act on the Word, all hell broke loose. It was bad enough trying to be nice to some of the membership but now this wet-nosed, young pastor was telling them they had to be nice and show compassion to all kinds of lowlives across Scranton. Plus, who did he think he was anyway? He might've had the title pastor, but at the end of the day, he was still their employee."

"So what happened?"

"Some of the more impressionable younger people actually believed the church would get behind the idea of showing compassion to the community. As a matter of fact, they created a Compassion for the Community ministry that went out and fed the homeless, worked in soup kitchens, and generally found a bunch of ways to show the love of Christ all across Scranton. I'm thinking you would have loved to be a part of that."

"Are you kidding?" Francine responded enthusiastically. "Oh my god. I would've been all over that. So what happened?"

"Well, after a while, the leadership just wasn't having it. The ministry kept coming to the church for money to fund things like free back-to-school supplies for poor black and Hispanic youngsters and snacks for after-school tutoring programs at the church."

"Maybe I'm missing something, Pastor," Francine said, "or maybe you're not telling it right. But I don't see how the leadership could find anything wrong with what the pastor was doing."

"Yeah, you would think so. But from what I heard, the Families were upset by the number of poor people and children coming in and out of the church's fellowship hall almost every day of the week and using up Redeeming Blood's food, water, and electricity. They complained that the poor and the indigent didn't support the church financially but were draining its resources."

"Now, I don't get that!" Francine said. "I'll be the first to admit that I'm not the brightest bulb on the tree. But I don't understand. How do you put a price tag on love and compassion?"

"Well, truth be told," he responded. "My understanding was, the Families weren't really concerned about the money. The game changer for them was the lack of control they had over the Compassion for the Community ministry. It had picked up momentum within Redeeming Blood and was revolving independently in its own orbit under the direction of this progressive young pastor."

"That ministry isn't here now, so something must've happened to it. What happened?"

Pastor Kidd uncrossed his legs, sat up in his chair and stroked his bald chin.

"It came to a showdown," he said somberly. "And as in most showdowns, somebody gets gunned down and somebody walks away. Well in this case, the ministry got shot down."

"Just like that?"

"From what I was told, the leadership demanded the pastor pull the plug on the ministry immediately. I don't know why they were surprised when he refused. I supposed they were not used to opposition. Long story short, the Families killed the ministry and fired the pastor. End of story."

"Are you kidding me?" Francine whispered loudly into both hands cupped against her mouth. "I can't believe people who call themselves Christians would be so heartless."

"Well, my dear, you'd better believe it. That's the flavor of Christianity they practice here at Redeeming Blood," Pastor Kidd said drily.

He looked at the clock on the wall behind Francine's head and realized it was almost two o'clock. He was usually home by then, lounging in his recliner in front of the family room's large-screen television. Since it was spring, he would give himself permission to sip a beer while watching baseball on television. Back in the day, he usually had a glass of Port or Kahlúa and cream in the colder months before Jennifer called him to dinner. She was probably wondering what was keeping him. So he abruptly stood up as a signal to Francine that their meeting was over.

But she gave no indication that she understood the pastor's nonverbal gesture. Instead, she crossed her legs at the ankles and leaned forward, revealing her two-color sneakers ensemble and reminding Pastor Kidd about their meeting's original purpose.

"Tell me something, Pastor," Francine said slowly, her forehead furrowed as if she were confronting some deep, mysterious phenomenon. "I'm a little confused, and I need you to help me to understand something."

"Sure," he said, as he walked to a built-in wall closet to retrieve his jacket. "I'll certainly try."

"Did you know all of this when you came here—what is it—three, four years ago?"

"I sure did," Pastor Kidd said, smiling as he pulled on his jacket. "I knew all about this church and about all the little peculiarities and eccentricities long before I sent in my resume."

"But I'm not understanding, Pastor," Francine responded, genuinely mystified. "Why in the world would you want to pastor a church that you knew had so much leadership issues?"

Pastor Kidd, who was already at the door, turned, walked slowly back into the room, and sat at the edge of his desk.

"Am I detecting a little hint of judgmental indignation here?" he asked serenely.

"No! Absolutely not, Pastor," Francine protested. "I'm just trying to understand why you would willingly walk into a volatile situation when you could've gone to any church in Scranton."

"Well, first of all, the only time there's a volatile situation at Redeeming Blood is when someone tries to disrupt the status quo. Other than that, things just move along as usual, and everyone's happy."

Francine shook her head in disbelief. She did not expect such a mollifying and despondent response. This was a man from whom she saw frequent moments of brilliance and profound intellect. She looked across the office at him, allowing Pastor Kidd to catch the depths of disappointment and frustration she felt at that moment. He saw the tears welling up in her eyes as she began to push herself out of the chair. He quickly returned to his chair, leaned over, patted the hand that was still gripping the arm of the chair, and motioned her to remain seated. For some unexplained reason, it suddenly became important that he not totally lose her approval or her respect.

"Look, Francine," he said, removing his hand but still leaning forward. "I'm sixty-five years old. And I had been an academic for most of my adult life."

"You are a college professor?"

"Well, I was, actually. I retired four years ago. May 15, 2010, to be exact."

"I'm not surprised you were a college professor. Where did you teach?"

"I was at Baptist Bible College and Seminary."

"Oh, really?" Francine said, smiling broadly. "That's so cool. I was thinking of taking some graduate classes there. Did you live up there in Clarks Summit?"

"Yes, we still do. We didn't see any reason to move after I retired. Plus, it's only twenty minutes from the church."

Eric Kidd had a relatively undistinguished record during his sixteen-year tenure at Baptist Bible College. He taught expository preaching, several levels of Greek, and pastoral counseling. And apart from attending the obligatory faculty meetings, he kept his head down and maintained the lowest profile he could muster. He limited his on-campus exposure to his office and to the classroom. Generations of students complained about his limited accessibility and the lack of any authentic advising he provided for the clubs and student organizations to which he was assigned. He attended a few conferences during his sixteen years at the seminary but only those within a two-hour driving range from Clarks Summit. His colleagues had long since stopped inviting him to their scholastic or social affairs.

It wasn't that he had an aversion to social or academic intercourse. Dr. Eric C. Kidd had been a rising star on the Christian seminary circuit for more than two decades. His area of expertise was the tension in the Black Church between Christian intellectualism and rural traditionalism. He was in great demand as a lecturer and presented papers at conferences throughout North America, the Caribbean, Europe, and Africa. He had published several articles each year in publications such as *Christian Scholar's Review*, *American Baptist Quarterly* and *Journal of Theological Interpretation*. When Kidd moved to the Baptist Bible Seminary, the expectation was that he might consider becoming editor of its publication, *Journal of Ministry and Theology*.

But he had put any hopes of continuing or expanding his scholarly career to rest by the time he arrived at Clarks Summit. By 1993, it was clear that Jennifer's diagnosis of chronic fatigue syndrome two years earlier would change their lives irreversibly. Because they had no children, their lives had become inextricably interwoven and interdependent.

Her Southern Christian fundamentalist parents had ejected her from the family because she refused to break up with Eric. They gave her an ultimatum during her senior year at Houghton College—a small Christian college in Houghton, New York, about an hour southwest of Buffalo. Jennifer's mother warned her she would have to renounce her African-American college boyfriend if she ever wanted to be welcomed back home in Edgewater, Alabama. And she knew she had accurately discerned the finality of her daddy's tone by the time he weighed in. There would absolutely be no acceptance of a black son-in-law in his world—ever. But Jennifer was surprised by her own tranquility and by the speed of her decision to choose Eric.

"It hurt a lot," she said over the years. "But I knew my parents, and I respected their decision. And yes, I missed them. But I couldn't imagine life without Eric."

There was never any bitterness about her parents' decision to erase their only child from their lives. Having lived the first eighteen years of her life in their world, Jennifer quite understood how racism could overpower love.

They got married in Houghton the day after they graduated. They married for pragmatic reasons and because they had become inseparable by then. Jennifer had no home or family to embrace her in Alabama. And Eric had no intentions of taking over his daddy's storefront church in West Philadelphia, as everyone had predicted since he was twelve years old. He actually loved the rigor of study and research. He grasped, even as a child, that there was no real glamor or gratitude in being a pastor. He knew, from experience, the emotional and financial toll on pastors and their families. He understood the liabilities of managing small high-maintenance churches. He recognized that the prominence and prestige pastors seemed to enjoy were illusionary.

Eric received a master's degree in theological anthropology at Eastern University and, later, a PhD in organizational leadership. Jennifer worked as an admissions counselor at the university, but she really lived for the evenings that merged into late nights when she helped Eric organize his projects and research material. It was a task she continued years later as Eric wrote and lectured extensively. They often joked that she earned the right to claim one half of his academic titles.

Eric and Jennifer were inseparable and seemed to enjoy the little bubble they had created for themselves. It was an exclusive space in which they allowed only a very select few. And as the demand for Eric's presentations grew, the admissions department allowed her to accompany him on his lecture tours across the country. It seemed that Christian intellectuals couldn't get enough of the apparent dichotomy that existed in what they previously considered as one of the most homogenous religious demographics. And for more than twenty years, Eric took enormous delight in exposing the myth of the Black Church as one big, monolithic spiritual, political, and cultural entity.

But by the spring of 1993, it was clear that Jennifer had lost much of her energy. Although her enthusiasm for supporting her husband never waned, it was evident that keeping up with the demands of his work was becoming increasingly taxing. Her favorite activities, such as strolling through town or working out in the campus gym, had become too exhausting. It turned out to be the initial onset of chronic fatigue syndrome, a condition that eventually grounded her from the activity she enjoyed most—assisting and accompanying Eric on his presentations. Still, she managed to help with some limited research and editing. However, even those activities ended after a while. Eric eventually curtailed his travels and limited his presentations to venues close to home.

Despite Jennifer's protests, Eric stopped traveling entirely when she was diagnosed with fibromyalgia in early 1994.

"I can't do it. I just can't do it," he told her. "It has always been the two of us from the beginning. We were a team. We are a team. My heart's not in it anymore without you."

Jennifer bitterly mourned the death of their working partnership. She felt the tremendous weight of guilt over grounding Eric's academic stardom. She blamed herself for injecting herself into his academic work. But she had inherited such rich insight into the traditions and peculiarities of the Black Church. Because of her years of research, Jennifer was convinced she understood better than most black people, the historical and cultural underpinnings of the several denominations that made up the Black Church. Maybe Eric interpreted her willingness to work so absorbedly with him over the years as the selflessness of love. But maybe what seemed as her sacrifice of time and energy was really her absolute insecurity and dependence on him all along. It could be that she was afraid to give herself the freedom to carve out her own career, so she chose an existence of vicarious achievements instead. At other times, she cried for the parents she lost and for the children she never had.

"So, is that when you moved to Baptist Bible Seminary?" Francine asked.

"Yes," Pastor Kidd said somberly, as if revisiting the distress of that time. "I took the college president up on an open invitation he made to me earlier. That's when we moved from Eastern to Clarks Summit."

"Did you ever regret it, Pastor?" Francine asked earnestly. "I mean, even today, after all this time."

"Honestly, I still miss the intense research. I miss collaborating with Jennifer. I miss the crowds. I mean, I miss it all. But let me be clear. I do not, for one minute, regret my decision. My wife means more to me than all of that. More than all the book sales, the fancy hotels or the lifestyle."

"Ooh. That's so sweet. You're making me cry."

"I mean it, though. There comes a time in our lifetime when we have to make choices. Hard choices. But it's a measure of our maturity when we pass up the expedient choices for the meaningful ones."

"So how is your wife doing?"

"Well, let's put it this way. She's the bravest, most resilient woman I know. But at the same time, I am her hands, feet and sometimes her voice."

"Lord, have mercy," Francine whispered, wiping her eyes with her sleeve. "I'll bet a lot of people don't know that about you."

"And there's no reason for them to know."

"I hear you," she responded. "So what happened at the seminary?"

"Well, I'm embarrassed to say not much." Pastor Kidd said, smiling. "I had to get used to teaching exclusively as a way of life. And it turns out, I didn't like it a whole lot."

"For real?" Francine asked with genuine surprise. "I would think coming from Eastern, you'd be the bomb."

"You'd think so. But I never got my groove at BBC. I'd do what I had to do in the classroom, in my office hours and at the insufferable faculty meetings. But I was always thinking about Jennifer and what she might be doing at home."

He said he knew that morally, he was doing a disservice to the college and to the students. But morals aside, he had to take a practical approach to the situation. He needed the health-care coverage the college provided them, pure and simple. He felt obliged to trade in his morality for pragmatism. Kidd had no illusions that the college granted him an assistant professorship with tenure based solely on his academic reputation. But after sixteen years of underachievement and reclusiveness, there were definite reciprocal yearnings for separation.

"Somewhere in all of this, I learned of Redeeming Blood." Pastor Kidd said. "I had visited a few times. Mostly just out of curiosity. I had heard that it was one of a few remaining *family-controlled* churches in the area. As a cultural and religious anthropologist, I was very curious about how the few descendants of a church's founding members were still able to exert the type of power necessary to control an urban church today. It was the kind of research I would do if I were writing a book in the future."

When he learned that Redeeming Blood had been between pastors for some time, he sent the leadership a carefully crafted letter listing his academic and scholarly achievements. He was confident someone there had at least heard of him during his heyday at Eastern. He was right. Not only had they heard of him but a few of them went out and bought copies of some of his books. Although, he seriously doubted they ever read past the dust covers. It took only one meeting with the church's pulpit committee and another with the joint board to know they had a deal. The joint board comprised of members of the deacon board and the trustee board. Membership to any of those bodies was based on some distinguishable link to Redeeming Blood's founding members.

The church's joint board had no concerns about his lack of pastoral experience. His daddy was a preacher. That was good enough. But his academic pedigree, they agreed, would work nicely for Redeeming Blood Baptist Church. His credentials would give them bragging rights across the city. That's because theirs would be the only church in the community that would boast of a pastor with an earned PhD. That had to be included on the sign outside. It would read, "The Reverend Eric C. Kidd, PhD, pastor." And that was money in the high-status bank.

But for his part, Pastor Kidd's contract stipulated he would receive a comparable package—with benefits—to what he was receiving at the seminary.

Although everyone in the meeting room was much too polite to mention it, both parties knew they came away with a bargain. For Eric Kidd, it was a generous benefits package with comprehensive health advantages. He wouldn't have to worry about any lapses in health care for Jennifer. And the joint board was giddy with excitement. They had bagged a nationally acclaimed Christian scholar for their pulpit. It didn't matter that he had not published or lectured in sixteen years. Plus, he went for the $95,000 salary and benefits package like a stray dog in a McDonald's dumpster. And they were prepared to go much higher. So when they slid a four-page contract over to him, he pretended to read it. Someone passed him a pen. And just like that, they had a new credentialed pastor, and he had a job with benefits. The board members were high-fiving and fist bumping around the table the moment Kidd left the room.

"Don't tell me God ain't good!"

"He's good all the time!"

"You got that right. He sent us just what we needed."

Meanwhile, Kidd strode out of the building toward the parking lot with an unholy smirk spread across his face. God just came through for him in a big way. It didn't bother him in the slightest that some of the contract's terms indicated that his major responsibilities would be preaching, teaching, baptisms, funerals, and baby dedications. Once he actually read the contract at home, it was clear that the church's administrative control rested with the joint board. He was, for all intents and purposes, a caretaker pastor.

That severely limited role might have bothered him earlier. But that evening, as he looked across the living room at Jennifer asleep on the sofa, Kidd felt no regrets about his decision. He looked at his wife with a mixture of sadness and brazen love. He grieved for her generosity of spirit and for her unsolicited affection. He missed her unbridled optimism and encouragement. He mourned the loss of her natural beauty. He always marveled at her ability to throw on anything and still manage to look radiant. But now, her once-golden hair was stringy and gray. The skin on her bare arms was now scaly and loose; her once-attractive face was now fixed into a permanent, painful grimace. His lovely Jennifer, who gave up everything for him, now depended on him for everything.

By then, Francine and Pastor Kidd were standing in the parking lot. His silver Dodge Caravan minivan and her yellow-and-black Mini Cooper were the only cars there. The sun was getting ready to dip behind a ridge of buildings bordering the fenced-in parking lot. But neither of them felt compelled to leave just yet. Both intuitively felt an impending moment of disclosure.

"So, is it safe to assume that this morning wasn't your best Easter service experience?" Pastor Kidd asked.

"Yeah, I guess," Francine responded. The memory of her embarrassment rushed back to choke her.

"Sister Francine," he began slowly, carefully. "I have to ask you. Why do you do it? Why do you put yourself through the ridicule and the intense scrutiny here? I mean, your style is your style. Your personality is uniquely yours. But why here at Redeeming Blood, of all places?"

"I know what you're saying. I know the people here don't get me. But I'm not here for them. I feel in my heart that God sent me here for a purpose."

"And do you know what that purpose is?"

"I didn't at first. But now I know. This is a big church with a lot of resources. But the resources are not used to benefit anybody outside the church. I believe God sent me here to make a difference. He sent me here to make this church minister to the community and to care for the poor and afflicted all around us."

"That's very interesting. But I'm curious to know how you're so certain that God led you here for that purpose. This idea of people being called by God has always fascinated me."

Francine told him that she moved to Scranton with her former boyfriend after she graduated from the State University of New York at New Paltz with a sociology degree. He moved back to New York after a few weeks but the United Neighborhood Center on Alder Street hired Francine as a housing coordinator. She immediately loved the challenge of finding permanent housing for homeless families and individuals. She never accepted the notion that the chronically poor and mentally disabled should remain invisible in the midst of opulence. She wanted to pull back the curtain on homelessness and reveal one of society's darkest secrets—blatant insensitivity to its most vulnerable population. And she found the ambivalence of faith-based communities to the homelessness most distressing.

Eventually, Francine felt led by God to infiltrate a church in the city with considerable resources and somehow help create a culture of concern for the homeless. That church would eventually become Scranton's catalyst for compassion. It was, at the very least, a sketchy plan. But Francine prayed earnestly for a sign from God that it was his will and therefore possible.

She visited several churches during that fall and winter of 2009 but always left feeling discouraged. Then she stumbled upon Redeeming Blood quite by chance one Sunday. The service had already begun, so the usher kept her in the vestibule for several minutes during the invocation. That was fine. Francine had visited enough churches by then to have a general sense of church protocol. But this usher seemed to have gone above and beyond her job description. First, she allowed the dozen or so latecomers into the sanctuary after the opening prayer but motioned for Francine to stay where she was. Then the usher had her stand there during the congregational hymn and until another collection of latecomers filled the vestibule. Meanwhile, she stared at Francine with unconcealed disapproval. She eventually directed another usher to show Francine up to the balcony.

But despite the usher's disrespect, Francine came away with the assurance that God wanted her to begin her work right there in the midst of that unfriendly environment. Her assurance came from Pastor Kidd's sermon. When the short dignified man with the head of wavy white hair stood up, she didn't expect much. He seemed like the typical black preacher, his black robe trimmed with red velvet running down the front almost touched the crimson-carpeted pulpit floor. The three red bars on each sleeve impressed her because she knew it was an indication that the preacher possessed a doctorate of some kind. Only a few of the preachers wore doctorate robes during her months of church visits.

But it was Pastor Kidd's message that fascinated her. He read from the Gospel of Matthew, chapter 25, verse 35 and 36.

> *For I was hungry and you gave me something to eat, I was thirsty and you gave me something to drink, I was a stranger and you invited me in, I needed clothes and you clothed me, I was sick and you looked after me, I was in prison and you came to visit me.*

Francine immediately felt spiritually transformed from the gallery of shame to which she had been banished, to being seated at the feet of the preacher. Although she had never encountered those verses before, she felt they were customized for her. She knew this was the sign God was sending her.

The preacher immediately told the congregation that Christ expected them to demonstrate their love for him by works of compassion for the disenfranchised, the poor, and the homeless.

"Homeless! He actually said *homeless*," Francine said aloud to no one in particular. But most people in the balcony looked in her direction. "I don't believe he actually said *homeless*. Wow!" she said.

She realized she had attracted everyone's attention upstairs, but it didn't matter. She had received her sign. She got up from her seat and moved to the front row, leaned forward, and rested her chin on the balcony rail. She didn't want to miss a beat.

The essence of the message, for her, seemed to be that Jesus expected his followers to minister to the less fortunate among them. These servants of Christ, the preacher said, were supposed to willingly provide for the basic needs of others after he left them. His followers did this even during times of personal danger to themselves. He said Christ's followers would eventually be persecuted. But he expected them, even then, to show their love and faith in him by their sacrificial provision to the poor. Pastor Kidd concluded that being charitable to the poor should not be an act of pity but an act of love. He said Christ regarded kindness to the poor as compassion they bestowed on him personally.

Francine sincerely believed she was hearing from God through the mouth of that distinguished, older gentleman. She couldn't believe the congregation was sitting so passively through such life-altering revelations. She heard herself yelling "Yeah!" and "That's true!" at the preacher. He even looked up and smiled at her a few times. *At least he knows someone is actually listening to his sermon,* she thought.

The usher caught up to Francine after the service at the bottom of the front steps and gently tugged on her sleeve. She wanted Francine to follow her off the slate walkway and onto the lawn adjacent to the parking lot.

"Miss, I know this was your first time here," the usher said through pursed lips. "I don't know if you're ever coming back. But if you do, I want you to know that we don't interrupt the pastor while he's in the pulpit. That's not the kind of thing we do here."

"Well, I'm sorry," Francine replied, although she sounded far from apologetic. "I just wanted the preacher to know he was speaking truth. That's all."

"I understand. But that's not done here. We're not that kind of church."

"Really? Then what kind of church are you?"

"Look, miss. We really don't have to take it there. I'm just telling you."

The usher abruptly turned around and marched back into the building, confident she would never see that hippie with the nose rings and tongue studs again.

But Francine was elated. She had received her sign from God. The Lord would use her in that stuffy church to open its doors to the poor and the homeless. And what better place to do it than to be at the door to welcome them in. It was so clear to her that God's plan was to use her to work alongside that same arrogant usher to open the church's doors to the least of his. She chuckled loudly as she got into her car, when she realized the persecution had already begun and she hadn't even started her ministry. But she felt a peaceful assurance that the Lord had already mapped out her course.

"You go, Jesus!" she screamed out the window as she tore out of the parking lot.

Pastor Kidd looked at his watch and realized it was almost three o'clock. He would have to get home soon to feed Jennifer. The residual heat on the asphalt from an exceptionally warm Easter Sunday was already cooling down. He thought he should hurry home to close the sunroom windows, where he had left Jennifer that morning. Maybe he would spend five more minutes with Francine before heading back to Clarks Summit. The traffic would be light that time of day. He could easily cover the approximately nine miles in about fifteen minutes.

"Oh, I see," he said. "You and Head Usher Angela Randolph had already met when you approached me about becoming an usher."

"Yes. You can say that."

"Uh-huh. I remember telling you to come see me after you completed your six weeks of new members' classes."

Pastor Kidd smiled as he recalled the unusual request he received from the peculiar-looking young woman after a Sunday worship service. He found it interesting that although she admitted she was unfamiliar with the concept of organized religion, she had always possessed a profound God consciousness. In addition, he found her determination to become an usher, as an integral part of her transition, pretty compelling. He had never before encountered anyone who viewed ushering as a divine call. That's why getting Francine accepted to the usher board was the only initiative, to date, that he had championed at Redeeming Blood.

However, he knew why the joint board grudgingly granted him that one-time dispensation to deferentially confront them. Allowing this new person to become an usher was a demonstration of the Families' power. But that reluctant approval concealed the hidden message that the pastor was never to attempt the implementation of any administrative or church policy initiatives ever again.

However, it wasn't long before the joint board regretted its rare decision of appeasement to the pastor by admitting the weird young woman to the usher board. The assumption that Francine would conform to the ushering norm by blending in proved to be unequivocally wrong. It took weeks of cajoling by Usher Randolph and her colleagues and the pastor's expert mediating skills to arrive at a compromise. Consequently, Francine agreed to give up her mismatched, eccentric ensembles when scheduled for usher duty. The concession was for her to wear the plain white usher's uniform if they would allow her to wear her Converse sneakers. Negotiations almost stalled until she agreed to wear only matching white sneakers with her uniform.

The only reason the ushers indulged Francine with the negotiations was because the Families instructed Usher Randolph to do whatever it took to make her an usher. That and because Irene King-Wheeler nodded in approval. Actually, nothing of significance happened at Redeeming Blood without her endorsement. And she exerted this significant influence without sitting on any church boards or participating in any meetings. But as the eldest descendent of the original six families, she controlled everything from the antique Princess phone on her nightstand. Irene King-Wheeler's granddaddy, Justus King, happened to be one of the church's original founders. And she never grew tired of hinting that Martin Luther King Sr. was her granddaddy's cousin. Mrs. King-Wheeler, who was portly and intimidating, possessed one of the few reserved seats in the sanctuary—fourth row, left side on the aisle. It was she who instructed the Families to honor their promise to Pastor Kidd this one time.

Francine, on the other hand, thought she had been negotiating from a position of strength. She presumed she had the pastor's support. And being under the impression that Pastor Kidd was the church's de facto chief operating officer, she expected his will to be their command. But unbeknownst to Francine, she was about out of bargaining currency with the Families. After almost three months as an usher, the leadership had had enough. Her weird sense of fashion embarrassed them. But more than that, the creepy class of people she attracted to Redeeming Blood offended them deeply.

Francine had walked Pastor Kidd to his minivan. He stood inside the opened door with one foot on the floorboard.

"Before I leave, I'm still a little confused," he said cautiously. "Would you mind if I asked you a personal question?"

"No, sir," she responded, smiling up at him. "Go ahead."

"Well, I'm still confused," Pastor Kidd began hesitantly. "You're an intelligent, young lady. You know the culture and tradition of this church. Why do you do it?"

"Why do I do what, Pastor?"

"Why do you continue to dress the way you do?" His voice was earnest, almost pleading. "Why do you insist on being so nonconformist? You must know it drives them crazy. But you seem to want to antagonize the very people with whom you're supposed to do worship and fellowship."

"Pastor," Francine replied, placing both hands on the van's opened window. "I'm not trying to antagonize anyone. Believe me. I don't know what it is, but ever since I was a little girl, I could never get down with the cutesy, frilly dresses my friends liked."

"Why, you preferred to wear pants?" he asked, betraying a hint of a smile.

"Naw. Now see where you going?" she responded, smiling back at him. "Naw, it wasn't like that. I wasn't trying to be a boy, if that's what you mean."

"I didn't think so," Pastor Kidd said.

"I don't know. I just liked making up my own styles. It was rough all through middle school because I had to put up with a lot of teasing and bullying. High school wasn't too bad though. I kinda hung out with other weird kids. Mostly Goths."

"So you never ever got dressed up in conventional or trendy dresses, slacks, regular shoes?"

"Yeah, I tried. In college, I joined the debate club as a freshman, and the coach insisted we dress up and look professional for the tournaments," she said, holding up air quotes. "You know, my roommate actually took me clothes shopping in a mall in Kingston. It was crazy."

"How did that go? Did you actually get dressed up for your grand debate?"

"Oh my god. This is so embarrassing," she said, giggling into her hands. "I never made it."

"How come?"

"I never told anyone this before. Not even my parents," she said, replacing her hands on the door window. "We were in Marshalls, I think. I took this whole bunch of dresses into the dressing room. I must've been in there a good half hour, trying on dresses."

"OK. So it took you a while to find what you liked. It happens."

"Not for me." This time her voice was subdued, almost sad. "I looked at myself in dress after dress. But I didn't see me. I saw this strange girl looking back at me. She didn't look real. Actually, she looked like a phony. And all the while, my roommate's telling me how 'this looks good' and 'that's the bomb.' But no matter how hard I tried to believe her, seeing myself in those dresses made me feel, I don't know, like bogus."

"Really?" he said. "So what happened with the debate tournament?"

"I don't know. I never went."

Over the next two weeks, a considerable amount of clandestine scurrying had been taking place behind the scenes at Redeeming Blood.

Members of the Women's Fellowship had been planning the annual pilgrimage to Central Baptist Church in Port Jervis, New York, for several months. The relationship between the sister churches extended back more than seventy years and had established the individual churches' Woman's Day as their most cherished events. The undercurrent of friendly rivalry between the churches over the decades gave the event high holy status.

The Port Jervis church billed their Women's Day activities as "An Evening of Elegance: The Women of Central's Tea and Worship Service." But the emphasis at both churches was always on the tea. It was evident because they put little effort into the worship service. For example, no one knew very much about the guest preacher for that year, except that she was once the pastor of a church in neighboring Middletown, New York. The attendees received their color assignments the previous year to ensure the entire assembly would be appropriately color coordinated. The color that year was purple.

The tea segment of the evening was supposed to replicate some long-ago period of formality and extravagance. Last year, Central's fellowship hall was ablaze in dusty rose and blue. The ceiling was almost obscured by networks of dusty-rose streamers and dangling blue buntings. Twenty round tables in the room were covered with the theme colors on alternate tables and decorated with elaborate floral arrangements and lighted, scented candles.

It was obvious the Central women were determined to outdo their Pennsylvania counterparts because they displayed new gold-plated silverware and new ivory-footed, cup-and-saucer, bone chinaware that year. The Central decorators placed impeccably folded twelve-inch blue linen napkins in the conventional position—to the left of the place settings. This was a subtle dig at their guests that Redeeming Blood committed an etiquette faux pas at their tea the previous year. Some of Redeeming Blood's napkins were in the middle of the place settings—an oversight Central's etiquette czar was happy to point out during the affair.

Normally, the Redeeming Blood charted bus would arrive at Central's parking lot not later than three forty-five. This gave them just enough time to empty the delicate treasures from their hatboxes, squeeze into their shoes and carefully inspect one another for any hint of imperfection. It was in preparation for the all-important grand entrance. The precision and execution of the procession from the bus to the fellowship hall took precedence over every other aspect of the evening. Although the procedure hadn't changed much in more than seven decades, the level of anxiety always remained high.

The women lined up alongside the bus, hidden from view of their hosts, who were straining from every available window to catch a premature glimpse of the cavalcade. The procession of forty-four women boisterously assembled themselves by height before stepping out from around the bus. After all those years, they couldn't decide who was taller than whom. Then at three fifty-five, they would march slowly toward the fellowship halls' side entrance, clutching their matching handbags under their outside arms. And following their tradition, the women at the head of the line would knock three times on the closed door. There would be a long pause before the door swung open to the rousing applause from inside the building.

The Redeeming Blood women would then parade down the aisle between the rows of colorfully decorated tables. Although everyone in the large room beamed, some were always overcome with emotion. They wept for deceased forerunners and for those too infirm to join them. Others shed joyful tears for the splendor of tradition. Marching into tea was carrying the torch of tradition into the future. It was their assurance that this sacred tea—this sisterhood bonding—would be kept intact for generations of Redeeming Blood and Central women. It was a treasured institution of church women who highly valued the occasional infusion of sophistication into their ordinary lives.

Repeated reminders for the Port Jervis tea circulated through the normal Redeeming Blood networks for months. Organizers took great pains to avoid general announcements for fear of attracting unsuitable elements—that would be new members or those the organizers believed didn't fit the mold. There were always forty-four women on that one-hour trip over the mountains to New York on Interstate-84. There were never additions—only replacements for death or infirmity. The replacements were quietly initiated into the tea sisterhood after detailed instructions in Victorian-era tea etiquette. And they were never allowed to forget what an extraordinary honor it was to be included into that privileged assembly.

But Francine got wind of the excursion somehow.

Some speculated that the pastor must have leaked the details to her. He, like most people who had been at Redeeming Blood for any time, knew about the reciprocal formal tea-and-service affairs between the sister churches. But they knew the value of staying in their lanes.

The chartered coach arrived promptly at two o'clock. Some women had been waiting in their air-conditioned cars in an attempt to keep their makeup intact. Others milled around the parking lot in little clusters close to individual mounds of shoe- and hatboxes, complimenting one another on their dresses and accessories. That section of the parking lot was awash in purple. Most of the women had already boarded the bus when

Francine's unmistakable Mini Cooper tore into the parking lot, pulled into the closest parking space and screeched to a stop. She tore across the space between her car and the coach within seconds and stood at the opened door breathing heavily. The remaining women waiting to board the bus gaped at Francine in disbelief and dismay. They couldn't believe she actually showed up to go to the tea. But her outfit was a definite jaw-dropper. She wore a royal-blue tank top over a full-length, purple, chemise skirt and purple, high-top Chucks. She pulled a purple beret out of a multicolored cloth shoulder bag and stuck it on her head as the final touch to her ensemble.

"Whew. I thought I was going to miss the bus for sure," she said breathlessly. "I wasn't sure if you guys were leaving at two or two thirty."

The three women looked at her, their eyes bulging in horror, as if a dozen bats were flying directly at them. They instinctively and in unison screamed out, "Mrs. King-Wheeler!" Within moments, the church's matriarch appeared at the top of the stairs, fully dressed except for her pink bedroom slippers and plastic shower cap. She peered down to the door at Francine standing in front of Sister Bernadette Simpson, Sister Andrea Vaughn and Sister Sybil Williams. Everyone on the bus was staring through a window to see what was happening outside. A few of them saw Irene King-Wheeler's already large frame expand as she grasped the reality of the situation on the ground.

"Oh, hell no!" she bellowed.

That was apparently the stimulus the women at the bottom needed. Sybil Williams, the youngest of the trio, stepped in front of Francine and attempted to elbow her away from the door. But as nimble and gutsy as a cornered cat, Francine ducked under her outspread arms and jumped onto the first step of the bus. The two other women slinked away with their hat and shoeboxes to a safer location. Irene King-Wheeler, meanwhile, clutched the metal rail that closed off the driver's cockpit with a beefy rings-bedecked hand. Meanwhile, she held up the other arm as if she were defending against a jump shot outside the paint. Francine, all frenzied energy by then, rushed up the steps to stand inches from her challenger. Her adrenalin, pumping at full blast, transformed her into a cyclone of aggression. She had only one objective: to find a seat. She was going to the tea, and nothing else mattered.

Francine bobbed to her right. She had slipped into basketball mode. Her opponent followed her movement and lurched sideways to block any advancement. But Francine swiftly changed her direction. The larger woman's body connected with empty space and crashed against the cockpit bar. Her hand simultaneously slammed on the horn in the center of the steering wheel. The horn blared deafeningly until Irene King-Wheeler's substantial body slid slowly and painfully to the floor. Francine nimbly stepped over the woman's exposed, outstretched legs and raced to the closest vacant seat, plopped down, and defiantly folded her arms.

The bus driver had been leaning against the parking lot's chain-link fence, smoking a cigarette. He immediately raced inside the bus when the horn sounded, stepped around Irene King-Wheeler's body, reached over to the dashboard, and shut off the engine. He was a small, olive-complexioned man with long, gray hair dangling from under his cap. He looked at the chaos in his bus and decided he did not want to know what was happening with those ferocious black women. He bounded off the bus as quickly as he got on, pulled out his cell phone, dialed furiously and resumed his place at the fence.

Meanwhile at the bus, several women were laboring to dislodge Francine from the seat. But she locked her arms around the back of the headrest in front of her, pressed her head against it and stiffened her body. They couldn't budge her. So, one woman grabbed her around her waist while another attempted to drag her off the seat by the feet. Several others were attending to Irene King-Wheeler, whom they eventually managed to raise to her feet and help her back to her seat. She had a substantial, painful bruise along her arm that stretched past her elbow.

"Get her off my bus!" Irene King-Wheeler screamed. "I want her off this bus!"

That spurred other women to join the two trying to dislodge Francine from the seat. But because of the limited space, they kept tripping and getting in each other's way. The woman in the next seat stood up and attempted to work her hands under Francine's armpits until she heard a ripping sound from a side seam and abruptly sat down. Everyone was out of their seats by then and squeezing toward the middle of the bus, where Francine had planted herself. They weren't sure how they were going to do it, but Mrs. King-Wheeler wanted the hippie-usher-girl off the bus. And they were going to get her off, somehow. The bus driver returned in the middle of the chaos and grabbed the intercom's microphone.

"Excuse me!" he bellowed into the microphone. "Excuse me!"

The bedlam gradually faded to a murmur. Everyone switched their focus to the front of the bus, although those holding Francine never relaxed their grip.

"I don't know what youse want to do," he said. "But it is now five after three. It takes at least a good hour to Port Jervis. If we leave now, we might still be a little late. What do youse want to do?"

Bedlam broke out again for several seconds until Irene King-Wheeler stood up with great effort. That's when those behind her noticed a broad black smudge at the back of her dress.

"Listen up!" she yelled. "Listen up!"

The bus immediately became silent. Every head turned in her direction, all eyes focused on her.

"We are going to Central Baptist Church today," she said slowly and with deliberate gravity. "You all know it's nothing but the devil trying to stop us, don't you? He sent this little demon straight from the pits of hell to get in our way today."

"Amen."

"That's right!"

"But the devil's a liar," she continued. "He can't stop this and that little bushy-head demon can't stop this neither. We been doing this before most of us were even born. We've come too far to turn back now."

"You know you right."

"The devil *is* a liar."

"You better believe it."

"So we going to stop all this devilish behavior right now," Irene King-Wheeler said, with the self-assurance of one who is used to exercising authority. "We are going to go to our affair as the dignified ladies we are. And we are going to leave now so that we will arrive on time. I've always said that it is rude and inconsiderate to be late."

"But what about *her*?" someone shouted from the back of the bus.

"Oh, don't worry about *her*," Mrs. King-Wheeler said. "She will not be permitted inside. If I know my sisters at Central, they are very selective and discriminating ladies. We all have designated places. They will have no room and no tolerance for people like *her*. Come, Driver, let's go. Get us there as quickly as you can."

She sat down abruptly, expecting the total compliance she received. No one offered to tell her about the huge stain at the back of her dress. The restraining hands brusquely released Francine, and the women returned to their seats. All eyes were on the driver as he slipped into the cockpit and pressed the starter button.

But except for two clicks, nothing happened.

The driver pressed the starter again. Everyone expected to hear the powerful diesel engine in the rear of the bus roar to life.

Click, click.

By now, the engine's silence caught everyone's attention.

"What's happening, Driver?" Irene King-Wheeler roared from directly behind the driver.

"You out of gas?" someone called out.

"Must be the battery. You run down the battery?" someone else offered.

He pressed the starter again.

Click, click.

"Why you doing that? You just running down the battery more."

The driver arose from the cockpit, retrieved his cell phone and dialed as he stepped off the bus. He walked to the rear of the bus and the women could hear him open and raise the hatch, exposing the engine. The commotion inside the bus had exploded into uncontrolled panic.

"How're we going to get there now?"

"I don't believe this."

"What piece of crap bus is this they send us?"

"You think we're going to miss the tea?"

"Yes! We're going to miss the tea. You really think they're waiting for us?"

"This don't make no kinda sense."

No one noticed the driver had reentered the bus until his voice crackled over the intercom.

"The garage says I have to let the computer reset itself before the engine will start again," he said.

"Reset itself?" Mother Bowden shouted out. "How long before it reset itself?"

"About twenty-five, thirty minutes," the driver said apprehensively.

The bedlam erupted again.

Eventually, Irene King-Wheeler's voice came over the intercom again.

"OK. OK. Let's calm down," she ordered. Silence immediately enveloped the bus. "Now, here is the reality. The bus wouldn't start for a good half hour. What that means is that there's a good chance we wouldn't make the tea."

A perceptible groan swept over the bus.

"So OK. We wouldn't get there in time for the tea. But we'll be in time for the service," she said. The resonance of her authoritative declaration and the finality of her statement suggested that she had accepted the situation, and it was now time for the rest of them to comply.

"Shoot, I don't care about no service."

There was a moment of shocked silence. No one had ever voiced the slightest opposition to a suggestion or decree from Mrs. King-Wheeler before. But no one claimed the statement.

"I didn't go through all this just for some service." This time, it was a voice from the back of the bus. "I always go for the tea."

"Me too" came from another voice on the other side. "I'm not trying to go all the way to New York just to hear some lady preacher preach."

"I agree. It's about the marching in and the tea for me. To me, the service is just something to do."

"Well, I don't know about nobody else but I'm taking my tired behind home."

At that moment, everyone on the stalled bus knew something significant had happened. The women felt that an important change had taken place. More than forty women had a spontaneous moment of defiance against the most prominent representative of the Families. It was an instinctive but irreversible act of rebelliousness that demonstrated the fragility of feudal domination. There was a sudden shift in the atmosphere. The mutual animosity over Francine and her unorthodox church attire gave way to the exhilaration for potential democratic freedom within the church. Maybe it was the image of their once-infallible leader lying on her backside, vulnerable and defeated. It could be that the conspicuous stain on her dress symbolized the actual vulnerability of the joint board and the Families she had led for so long.

But one by one, the women gathered their hat and shoeboxes and silently left the bus for their parked cars. They walked past Irene King-Wheeler without any acknowledgement. She remained in her seat, looking dazed and defeated. She was trying to process what had happened and how she would explain this rebellion on her watch to the other joint board members. She was pragmatic enough to recognize the beginning of an insurrection.

She realized, after a while, that she and Francine were the only ones on the bus. Although she hated sharing any space with that disruptive troublemaker, Irene King-Wheeler realized she didn't have the energy or the desire to step off the bus. The minute she did, she would be stepping into the new reality—a changing of the guard at Redeeming Blood Baptist Church. She closed her eyes, and in the stillness of the bus, she heard Francine shuffling down the aisle toward her.

"Oh, well," Francine said cheerfully. "If I leave now, I can make it to Port Jervis before the service begins. Shoot. Somebody's got to represent. I'll give them your love."

# # #

REVIEWS FOR

Stories from the Pews

If the call to preach has ever baffled you, *Trial Sermon* from *Stories from the Pews* gives a compelling view of the mystery through wit, humor and lived experiences, providing a glimpse along the way of complex family dynamics, *church* antics and life choices. I laughed . . . I cried . . . I understood.

—Rev. Dr. Faye Banks-Taylor, director, New York Campus, New Brunswick Theological Seminary, pastor, St. Mark's Chapel AME Church, Kingston, New York

The characters from Dr. Modele Clarke's short stories, jump out at you as someone from your church, school, or job. The stories are so imaginatively well written that it's difficult to read fiction into what is *so imaginably real.* Dr. Clarke's book of short stories is definitely one to grace the book shelves of avid readers at home, at the office, or even *in the pews at church.*

—Dr. A. J. Williams-Myers, professor emeritus, Black Studies Department, State University of New York at New Paltz

Rev. G. Modele Clarke paints a vivid picture of Black Church life with his brilliant collection of stories. He is a skillful storyteller and his descriptions of the characters allow you to become part of their lives. You are transformed from a passive reader to an active participant in their stories. You root for Reggie to take over and preach and prove his grandmother wrong; you want Francine to triumph over the haughty women on the usher board; and you cheer knowing that Rosalie will finally be free of her tyrannical husband. My only regret in reading these stories is that they ended.

—Dr. Janis Peters, professor,
Program for Advanced Learning,
Curry College, Milton, Massachusetts

Printed in the United States
By Bookmasters